THE DUFORT DYNASTY
BOOK ONE

BY JULIETTE N. BANKS

COPYRIGHT

Author: Juliette N. Banks

Editor: Inked It Out Editing

Cover design by: Elizabeth Cartwright, EC Editorial

ABOUT THE AUTHOR

Juliette is an indie steamy romance author who has taken the paranormal romance genre by storm with her popular vampire series, The Moretti Blood Brothers. Not all of her sexy and powerful heroes are supernatural—Juliette now has a series of hot, page-turning contemporary romances readers can't get enough of.

Juliette also has a vast background in consumer marketing and previously published with Random House. She lives in New Zealand with Tilly, her Maine Coon kitty.

www.juliettebanks.com

DEDICATION

I dedicate this book to summer.

You are my favorite season of the year. I love the delicious heat, long balmy nights, pretty flowers, swaying palm trees, singing birds, sand between my toes, and suntans.

Not the mosquitos though—I want that on record!

I wrote Sinful Duty outside on my deck in the heat of summer in Auckland, New Zealand. Perhaps that's why I based this story in Hawaii?

Either way, I hope it brings warmth to your heart and you love Harper and Daniels' love story.

Juliette x

ALSO BY JULIETTE N. BANKS

The Dufort Dynasty
Steamy billionaire romance
Sinful Duty
Forbidden Touch
Total Possession

The Moretti Blood Brothers
Steamy paranormal romance

The Vampire Prince
The Vampire Protector
The Vampire Spy
The Vampire's Christmas
The Vampire Assassin
The Vampire Awoken
The Vampire Lover
The Vampire Wolf
The Vampire Warrior

Realm of the Immortals
Steamy paranormal fantasy romance
The Archangel's Heart
The Archangel's Star
The Archangel's Goddess

SINFUL DUTY

CHAPTER ONE

Daniel Dufort lifted his whisky to his lips and nodded at the blonde who was regaling him with an apparently *hilarious* story of her father at their recent New Year's party.

Daniel knew who the man was. The fact he'd actually spent time with his wife and family was a small Christmas miracle. He'd heard rumors—and his source was pretty reliable—that her father, Senator Johnson, had two girlfriends. Neither of which knew about the other. With Valentine's Day approaching, it would be an expensive one for the politician.

Three women. *Ugh.*

Daniel shivered at the thought. He preferred his women in and out in an evening, not sticking around for breakfast or a ring on their fingers.

He glanced around *Bar Hugo*, one of Manhattan's most exclusive bars, and saw most of his key connections had now left. The only reason he was still nursing his Macallan was, to put it bluntly, his cock. The blonde, who wouldn't stop talking, was going to have her mouth around it within the next hour.

Beep, beep.

Daniel, we need to speak. Meet me in your office in an hour.

After reading his father's message, he mentally rearranged his plans. Dropping his crystal glass onto the polished wooden bar, he replied to confirm he'd see him there, and then took the petite blonde's arm. "Shall we go?"

Her face lit up.

"Your place or mine?" she purred.

"I have a meeting in my office tonight, so let's head there," he replied, leading her to the private exit. The last thing he wanted was to be photographed with her and more gossip spread about his relationship status.

When would the media give up? He was never getting married.

She hesitated slightly as his offer sank in. There would be no breakfast in bed. Daniel held her gaze. The decision was hers—she could take it or leave it.

He knew she'd take it.

They all did.

A billionaire in a suit was an aphrodisiac to these types of women.

Like his brothers, he had inherited their father's good looks. At six foot three with a muscular frame—which he worked hard to maintain in his gym—and a square jaw, Daniel was confident and powerful.

Some of it learned. Some of it was natural.

In the United States, and other places around the world, Daniel Dufort was frequently quoted in business and economic media, and unfortunately in less respected publications for the women he took to events. Rarely, if ever, was it the same women, and yet they insisted on discussing his marital status.

The gossip columns had a few cringeworthy nicknames for him. Try as he may, Daniel struggled to keep his sex life private. He only had a few rules.

No promises.

Nothing overnight.

No, do overs.

Okay, fine—he occasionally slept with the same woman twice, but not in the same quarter or it gave the wrong impression.

Daniel Dufort wasn't interested in a relationship. Of any kind. He didn't believe in true love, nor was he going to settle for something vanilla. However, he did enjoy female company, and the activities at the end of the evening, so he took dates to the events he had to attend, or to meet some social obligation.

And he wasn't lacking in options.

But a relationship was not for him.

Settling down with a *best friend* and having missionary-style sex three times a week? No thanks.

As predicted, she'd walked through the door, so they head to Dufort Towers. Daniel hung his dark gray Tom Ford jacket on the hanger and turned.

Miss Johnson—*fuck, he'd forgotten her name*—lingered, taking in the valuable 57th Avenue view that overlooked Central Park. It was one of the best along Billionaire Row.

"Stunning," she said, stepping up to the full-length glass.

Daniel removed his cufflinks, and they pinged as he dropped them on his custom-made oak wood desk. He rolled his shirt sleeves to his elbows and checked the time on his Piguet watch.

They had thirty-five minutes.

Daniel moved to stand beside Miss Johnson and dug his hands in his pockets. "I'm going to assume you give head."

She turned, her mouth opening.

A good start.

Daniel leaned in and ran his finger through her hair. "Or I can bend you over my desk and fuck you. You decide."

Her mouth closed and acceptance settled over her features. She was too proud to storm out, and he knew she was wet for him.

She reached for his fly and slid to her knees. "Both." Her eyes lifted to his as she gripped his cock.

Daniel didn't answer. He simply watched her tongue swirl around his swollen head and take him deeper, inch by inch.

Daniel let out a low moan. He gripped her hair and pressed in further while she moved skillfully over and around him. It wasn't long before he was fucking her throat as she milked him dry. He groaned out his orgasm while she swallowed.

That was a bonus—he thought she'd be a spitter.

She sat back on her Manolo Blahnik heels and licked her lips. She was a beautiful woman, more natural than many in this town, but like all those before her, Daniel suddenly lost interest.

Most of them were here for his last name. They often had trust funds or money of their own, but he had power and they falsely believed by marrying him, they would also have power.

They were wrong. Power was someone either had or didn't have. It came from within, as much as a bank balance.

Dufort Hotels, which made up most of the Dufort Dynasty, had properties all over the world. It had been built by his father and went public five years ago. Two years ago, his father had stepped away—though remained the majority shareholder—and Daniel had taken on the position he'd been groomed for all his life.

CEO of Dufort Hotels.

"Thank you for being my date tonight," he said, zipping his pants. God, why could he not remember her name? Megan. Shit. "Give your father my regards, Megan."

She stood and smiled at him, all sultry. "I think you've forgotten about part two."

No. He hadn't.

Fortunately, his father was always early and at any moment he'd be interrupted if things got tense. Occasionally, claws came out when they felt rejected.

"Looks like we are out of time. I need to prepare for my meeting," he replied with no pretense of disappointment, then stepped away. "Please make use of the facilities before you leave if you need to."

Daniel stepped behind his large desk and lifted his laptop open.

Megan cleared her throat and picked up her purse. "No, thank you. I will gargle the sperm from my throat with a glass of *Cristal* champagne when I get home," she replied, then spun and walked out of the office with her head held high.

Despite himself, Daniel smiled.

Good for her.

A moment later, his father stepped into his office, thumbing his finger over his shoulder. "Was that Senator Johnson's daughter I saw leaving?"

"Yes. She accompanied me to the *Glass Towers* rebrand launch this evening," Daniel said.

Glass Towers were a friendly competitor in New York City, but a competitor, nevertheless. He'd chosen the senator's daughter as a political statement because of some government lobbying he was doing regarding the water system in Manhattan. The CEO, David Glass, disagreed with Dufort, which could cost *Glass Towers* a small fortune if it went ahead. But it was the right thing to do, and they both knew it.

Daniel smiled. He loved the game, and he was good at it.

Johnathan Dufort walked over to the same spot Megan had *performed* in and rocked on his feet. It wasn't unusual for them to meet in the evenings, but Daniel knew what this was about. It had been a hot topic for weeks and was his least favorite subject right now.

"I don't have good news, son," he said. "The agreement is still missing and now Senator Mackenzie is trying to extort us."

He looked up.

"With what?" Daniel asked loudly. "He's already doing that by claiming we owe him more interest on the initial loan than was originally agreed to."

Nearly two decades ago his father had entered an agreement with his then friend, Bill Mackenzie. The amount had been substantial—in the high six figures—and was paramount in Dufort Hotels growing into what it was today. The loan was to be repaid in twenty years with three percent interest.

It was no secret. Their finance team had been putting the money aside over the years and were preparing to pay it out in this financial year.

A few weeks ago, they'd received a letter from the *now* senator requesting payment for a much larger sum. Attached was a copy of the agreement.

Except it wasn't the original—it had been doctored.

The three percent interest had ballooned to *fifteen* percent. A rate no one in their right mind would agree to.

Very few people were aware of the situation, outside his father, his brothers Fletcher and Hunter, their financial advisor and lawyer. The latter had advised they hunt down a copy of the agreement before going to the authorities.

Johnathan Dufort had thought he had a copy at home in his own files, along with the one kept in the vault at Dufort Dynasty.

Apparently not.

His father ran a hand over his face.

Shit.

"Father. Tell me."

Johnathan slammed his fist down onto the arm of the sofa next to him. "He's said we have thirty days to pay, or he wants his daughter married into the Dufort family. The prenup cannot exclude her from the Dynasty shares."

"You have got to be fucking kidding me," Daniel growled.

He knew what was coming next.

"She has asked for you."

CHAPTER TWO

Daniel cursed.

He slammed the door of his office and directed his father to sit. Things had gotten completely out of hand.

"I'm not marrying Nadia fucking Mackenzie."

His father crossed his arms. "Of course you don't want to marry her. That's not what this is about. They're blackmailing us. Unless we find that document, we're fucked."

Jesus.

There had to be a way out of this.

Daniel had been CEO now for two years and every day he woke up feeling like he was living the dream. He was a rich and powerful man, proud of their hotels and the type of employer they were. He'd do anything for the business and his family.

But allow himself to be blackmailed into marrying Nadia Mackenzie?

No.

Fuck that.

His father might believe they were fucked, but Daniel would not sit back and sign his life away to a cold, boring woman—because, yes, he knew Nadia and he'd nearly fallen asleep during both the conversations he'd had with her.

It wasn't just that—Daniel had no plans to marry anyone. Ever.

Hell, after witnessing his parents' divorce as a teenager, Daniel had quickly decided it wasn't for him. All three of the Dufort brothers had watched their mother slowly become an alcoholic while his father worked twelve to eighteen-hour days—three of them spent fucking other women.

Sure, he had a healthy sex life, but Daniel wasn't a cheater.

His mother had eventually figured it out. Her tears had turned to anger, bottles were thrown, and vases smashed. When she'd ripped up a valuable painting and left it at the entrance of their Park Avenue penthouse, his father had filed for divorce.

Marie Dufort was moved into an apartment a few blocks away and saw the boys only on weekends. She was now a recovered alcoholic who Daniel spoke to a few times a month.

So, while his father built the Dufort empire and bent secretaries over his desk, and his mother drank herself stupid, the three boys had emotionally been on their own.

There had been no one to console him after he'd had a fight with Timmy on the playground—which he'd won—or explained why Suzie had passed him a note with a flower drawn on it. Then cried when he screwed it up because it seemed dumb. Or why, when he'd had his first kiss, he'd felt all weird on the inside.

They'd only had each other and because of that, all three of them were close. Which served them well now as business partners. Hunter was the Director of Sales and Fletcher the Director of Marketing and PR.

"Then it's time we talk to Brent about speaking to the cops," he said, referring to their company lawyer.

His father frowned at him like he was an idiot.

"Daniel, he's a damn senator. They'd laugh us out of the station," Johnathan said.

Yeah, he knew that. Without proof, they didn't have a leg to stand on.

"And you have no idea who could've taken these copies? Because it should be in the damn vault, Dad," he asked, using the familiar term which he rarely did at work. "And are you sure you had a copy at home?"

His father turned, then shook his head.

"No. I'm not sure about the second copy. Damn it. It was twenty years ago, son! I went to Harvard with the son of a bitch. I never in a million years thought he'd pull something like this. I've known him for two decades."

Daniel nodded.

The two men weren't best friends, but they were both professional, successful men who'd made a sound business agreement.

Johnathan could have gone to the bank twenty years ago and borrowed for a better rate, but they wouldn't have loaned him the full amount. Bill had inherited millions from his grandfather and was looking for a long-term investment with a good return. Dufort Hotels had appealed to him.

He was right.

"Of course we have the money, but I'm not fucking giving it to him," his father said.

Dufort Hotels was a thriving hotel business worth billions of dollars. They had seventeen hotels in seven countries around the world. As the CEO, he knew about every loan, deal, and project in the organization.

"No, we're not paying him. We're fucking Dufort's. We do not pay blackmailers, no matter what the title before their name is," Daniel growled. "Nor would the board agree to this."

Hopefully, they'd never find out either.

Something like this could seriously destabilize them and affect their share price. Unless he found a way out of this, he may have no damn choice but to marry Nadia.

Could he actually go through with it? Daniel ran his hand through his dark, wavy hair, fighting the urge to punch a wall.

"God damn it, I'm not marrying Nadia."

"Twenty fifth of February, the senator is announcing the engagement if the payment is not made."

Daniel shook his head.

He was going to find a way out of this. He had a number on his phone he was calling as soon as his father left. Someone who could find things out, working a little outside the law. Someone you wanted on your team when you were being royally screwed.

But it was going to cost him.

"Daniel, we need to be prepared for this, not to go our way."

My way, you mean. I'll be the one saying wedding vows.

He ground his teeth.

"I'll get my lawyers drafting a prenup while I'm on the islands." Daniel said.

He was flying to Hawaii the next day. Fletcher had been approached by a production company about filming in their hotel and, unfortunately, the timing conflicted with a medical procedure.

He'd asked Daniel to go on his behalf.

It was no secret their Waikiki hotel was one of his favorites, and Daniel had mentioned wanting to be more visible around their regions now he was in the top job. Plus, he was looking forward to getting away from the snow New York City was known for in February.

Unless a miracle occurred, he would return to Manhattan preparing to marry a woman he could barely stand.

Hopefully, the Obamas would be in residence in Hawaii, and hosting a party or two. A few sexy distractions sounded pretty good about now.

CHAPTER THREE

Harper Kāne twisted in her seat. The nine-hour flight to Hawaii from Auckland wasn't the longest she'd ever done, but tonight she just couldn't get comfortable. It didn't help that she'd fallen asleep in the sun that afternoon, so she was a little pink. It was mid-summer in New Zealand and theirs was an unforgiving sun—even with olive skin.

Despite her Hawaiian heritage from her dearly departed father, Harper had only visited the tropical islands twice before. She'd fallen in love with the tropical paradise and had chosen it as the location for her popular fiction series.

Harper had been writing for three years now and readers loved her books. While she wasn't the next *J. K. Rowling—yet*—things were looking up. She'd recently left her corporate job to write full-time, which was a wonderful accomplishment.

Unfortunately, the exciting life milestone, marked only three months ago, aligned with another major life change.

Her fiancé, David, who'd never been supportive of her writing, had asked her not to quit. They'd argued about it, despite Harper showing him her consistent and rather healthy income.

At the time, she was exhausted working a full-time job, while writing another twenty hours every week. Harper knew it was the right thing to do for her health, her business, and that the risk was low.

David disagreed.

He just didn't believe authors could earn a living from writing *silly books.* He thought she was being irresponsible, and it would impact them buying a house together.

Harper had been torn and put off her decision for a few weeks. It was funny how life nudged you in the right direction anyway. A few days later, her boss told her they weren't replacing the colleague who had recently resigned, and that her workload would be doubling.

Harper had quit on the spot.

She knew David would be mad, but she was determined to back herself and show him there was nothing to worry about. It wasn't like she'd run away to join the circus.

Turns out Harper had been right about one thing: David had been furious.

For two weeks, he barely spoke to her. Then one Saturday afternoon she returned from the mall and found David and all his belongings gone. After five years together all he'd left was a note which said: *I just can't trust you anymore. David.*

Which was ironic because she found out a few weeks later he'd moved in with Jenny, the single blonde sales rep David worked with. The one who always flirted with him at work functions, and Harper was told she was being *dramatic* about.

Right.

Harper had been shocked and heartbroken. Then furious. Then sad. And all the other emotions in between. She'd called her mom and best friend Kristen and they'd shown up with tubs of ice cream, pizza, and vodka.

Though she wanted her mom's loving arms around her, Harper had gritted her teeth most of the evening as the woman reiterated that men were not trustworthy.

She had good reason to feel like that, but not *all* men were bad.

Were they?

Her mother had met and fallen in love with Harper's father in Hawaii, then convinced him to move to New Zealand when they got pregnant with her. They had married quickly. Her father had never settled completely, going back and forth to the islands, sometimes staying for months at a time.

It had been hard for Harper not having her father around and hearing her mother crying to him on the phone. Finally, when she was old enough, she realized there were other women. Worse, when she was thirteen, they discovered he had a whole other family in Hawaii.

It had been devastating.

Now she understood her mother's anger and pain. Her mom had vowed to never trust another man again, remaining angry and on her own.

Was that the path Harper was on now? She liked to think it was temporary and one day she would move on.

Harper had traveled to Hawaii to see her father and meet her *other* family. She resented them immediately when she saw their home and how engaged he was in their life. He had never been like that with her and her mom. Three months after her visit, her father had suddenly died of a heart attack.

Harper and her mother traveled back to Hawaii for an awkward as hell funeral, and that was the last she'd seen of her half siblings.

Now, here she was, going back to the tropical island.

After David, or AD, as she liked to refer to it as, Harper had got busy writing and marketing her books. She was determined to make a success of it and prove herself. Suddenly, seven weeks ago, she was approached by a leading network, *BookFlix,* who wanted to produce her romance series, *Island of Tomorrow.*

Yes! she'd said after negotiating and working out the final details.

Kristen had dragged her out to a local bar where they had gotten completely smashed and danced like idiots all night long. It was just what Harper had needed.

Now she was on her way to Hawaii to meet with the team to look at locations and prepare for filming later in the year. She'd asked to be as involved as possible to ensure her books were represented accurately.

Harper had two weeks on the island, giving her a few days before the network arrived, then a week after her business with them was complete.

"I really wish I could afford to come with you," Kristen pouted for the third time during their drive to the airport.

"Me, too." Harper had tried to justify spending the money to take her friend with her, but flights from New Zealand were costly and they'd both agreed they'd plan a proper girls' holiday one day in the future.

"Find yourself a sexy Hawaiian boy, or man in uniform, while you're there and have some sexy fun," Kristen said, winking.

Harper shook her head. "Hell no. Either I have poor taste in men or bad luck. I'm going to shop, read, swim, tan and surf—not in that order—and that's it."

And focus on her books being turned into an amazing show for her readers. She couldn't wait to tell them.

Her heart was still pretty bruised. She knew now David wasn't the one, but the way he'd left had been cold and cruel.

It was clear he was cheating on her, or about to, and had used her career change as an excuse, manipulating her as he did.

Asshole.

It had taken a lot for her to open up and trust him when they'd first met. She had just turned twenty. On her twenty-first birthday, he'd pushed for them to move in together and then two years later he had proposed.

Had Harper burst into tears and said yes? No. She had asked for a few days to think about it. Which should have been a sign.

But after watching her parents' marriage, Harper wouldn't race into anything. Her mother was constantly in her ear about David and how she shouldn't trust him.

Turns out she had been right.

So, no, Harper had no intention of letting another man into her heart or life. She just wanted to focus on her career, and she'd worry about what that meant another day. She was only twenty-five—she had her whole life ahead of her. One that didn't include lying, cheating men.

"Such a waste," Kristen said. "Look at you— you're God damn gorgeous. All that olive skin and gorgeous long, dark hair."

Harper knew she had been blessed with her father's Hawaiian genes and her mother's fast metabolism. However, she also worked out regularly and ate healthy. Tomorrow she would confidently put on a bikini and step onto Waikiki Beach.

"That doesn't mean I should go around sleeping with all the men on the island." She laughed.

"Not all of them. Two or three would be sufficient." Kristen had shrugged and given her a cheeky grin. "And let that hair of yours down—my God, girl, you have the gifts. Use them."

Harper's hand lifted self-consciously to her long, dark curls, which David had called a permanent mess. Perhaps that was why she always wore it up in a bun or some other twist.

He was right, though. Even when she did that, strands would come loose.

"Later, or it will frizz on the plane."

"I think I need to buy a ticket. You are going to waste this trip. You need to be young and stupid—even for one of your two weeks."

Harper shook her head and laughed.

She was very clear about her goals in Hawaii. A holiday romance was not one of them.

CHAPTER FOUR

Daniel wandered through the lobby of Dufort Waikiki nodding and acknowledging the *Aloha, Mr. Dufort* greetings.

He'd flown into Oahu on his private jet the day before, arriving early evening. It had been a restless trip.

He'd reluctantly drafted an email to his lawyers asking them to draw up a prenup. It was better to be prepared, even though he hoped this was a precaution.

Duke Johnson had video called him just before they landed. "What the hell? Is this serious, or are you messing with me?"

"Do I ever joke around about my money?" Daniel had asked in response, arching his brow.

"Jesus," his lawyer of the past ten years had replied.

Once he'd updated Duke with as much as he could share, the man had shaken his head. "What a fuckup. Okay, I'll get something drafted and send to you in a few days."

"I don't want anyone else working on this. Fuck the client privilege bullshit, this has to remain high level." Duke was an owner and partner at his firm and his rates reflected it. Daniel was happy to pay the big bucks, even for something as simple as a prenup. Not that it was a problem for a man with the type of wealth he had—but he wasn't risking anyone finding out about this.

"Yeah, of course, Daniel. I'll get something to you in the next few days so you can speed things along at your end."

He didn't want to speed things along.

He didn't want to get married.

To Nadia or anyone.

"Like I said, it's just a precaution. I'm hoping to sort this out."

"How?" Duke asked. "Sounds like Mackenzie has you over a damn barrel."

Yeah, he did.

"I may have been born with a silver spoon in my mouth, but I also shoot with silver bullets, Duke. Never forget that."

When had he given anyone the impression he took shit lying down? He wasn't known as a soft touch in business, and that wasn't about to start now. Extortion or otherwise.

His lawyer stared at him for a long moment.

"Yeah, all right. Just be careful. I might be your lawyer, but God, don't tell me anymore. I'm not saying I don't want to see the asshole taken down a notch, though."

Daniel breathed in the scents of his Waikiki hotel. There was something unique about it which always felt happy. Hell, it was Hawaii. How could it not be?

"Good morning, Mr. Dufort," a Dufort staff member greeted him.

"Aloha," he said, nodding with a small smile. He felt like punching a wall, but there was no reason to let his employees see that.

Perhaps when his contact at the private security firm returned his call, he'd feel more in control. Because if someone was trying to fuck him over, he was more than happy to do the same in return.

You had to fight fire with fire.

And *Black Hawke Security* was packing. Sometimes literally. They were a bunch of former-Marines. Black ops. That kind of crew. In fact, Josh Hawke was a former Navy SEAL. Daniel knew enough about the guy to know he was a wealthy mother fucker because of his grandfather's investments. He'd left the SEALs and started *Black Hawke Security* with Aidan Black.

Hence the name.

They were the go-to guys when shit got ugly.

They had contacts and access to things the law didn't, or couldn't, touch to get the job done.

Daniel had reached out to them about a few small jobs, but nothing this sensitive.

Because Mackenzie was a fucking senator.

He was unsure whether Josh or Aiden would even touch this job. Then again, this was their specialty, so he hoped like fuck one of them returned his call soon.

"Aloha, sir," Akino, the general manager of Dufort Waikiki, said. "How was your first night?"

Daniel rarely traveled, so his visit was causing a stir.

"Aloha, Akino. It was excellent. The suite is looking good," Daniel replied, shaking his hand. "Do we have the meeting rooms booked as discussed for later this week?"

Akino nodded.

"Yes, *BookFlix* arrives in three days. The large conference room has been set aside for you. It can be turned into two or four private spaces if necessary."

Ah yes, the electronic moving walls they'd updated to a few years ago—it had increased their revenue in the conference space by thirty percent. Ingenious technology.

"Are they staying in the hotel or elsewhere?" Daniel asked.

"Here, sir."

"Good, good."

"Also, the author," Akino said.

"Author?"

"Yes, sir. The author. She wrote our—*your*—hotel into her books and is apparently consulting on the project while they're here."

Daniel stared at the man, wondering if it was necessary for him to know this author or the books. "Which books? Should I be familiar with them?"

Akino blushed. "Ah, the um, *Island of Tomorrow* series. They're tropical island romance books. Very popular."

Christ.

"Have you read them?" Daniel asked, attempting to keep judgment from his voice.

"Well, you know, because she mentions our hotel, so I skimmed through them," Akino said, shrugging.

Liar.

Daniel nearly smirked.

"Are they those book porn romances women now read?" Daniel asked.

Akino laughed. "Yes, sir."

He rolled his eyes. The author probably needed to get laid if she spent her days writing that rubbish. "So the author will join the meeting with the network?"

"Yes. Harry, our new marketing manager, will attend with you and manage most of the operational side of things. And of course we will be directed by you on anything to do with reputational risk and PR."

Daniel nodded.

"Fletcher will pick this up with Harry once he's back at work next month."

Daniel didn't mind getting involved with some of the details some days. Being CEO meant he had a big picture view of the company and was rarely hands on anymore. Ultimately, he was responsible for everything, including reputation, which right now was more at risk than anyone knew.

"Yes, sir. Harry will work with the local teams here to reduce the interruption to our guests during production and ensure there is good communication to local authorities in and around the area."

Daniel nodded.

He had no doubt in the efficiency of his team, but Harry was a new employee, and he didn't want to go into a meeting with a big organization like *BookFlix* unprepared on any level.

"Set up a meeting with Harry for this afternoon," Daniel instructed. "Tell him to walk me through his plan and any concerns or thoughts."

Akino nodded, and jotted down notes into his tablet, then looked up at his silence.

"Don't scare him. I just want to go in prepared knowing who the people on my team are," he added.

Akino smiled at him.

He'd known the Hawaiian man for nearly ten years. Johnathan had taken Daniel on a global tour of all their hotels in his early twenties and he had spent a week here learning the ropes.

Akino had been younger, of course, and had shown Daniel around. It wasn't like they had become friends—Daniel was always a Dufort and was treated as such—but over the years, they'd both seen each other grow up.

"He's very competent. I'm sure you will be impressed."

"I don't doubt it," he said, inadvertently complimenting Akino.

Daniel's eyes tracked across the hotel lobby and landed on a pair of tanned legs. Even before his eyes reached her perfect c-cup breasts or her luscious long, dark wavy hair, his cock reacted.

Jesus.

He felt like a fucking teenager.

Down boy.

The woman was dressed in a bright pink bikini with a pair of denim shorts and black flip-flops. On her shoulder, she carried a beach bag with a towel poking out. She lowered her sunglasses as she neared the entrance, ready to step outside.

"Right, well, I think—" Akino said, then called out, "Oh, look, here's Ms. Kāne!"

The sexy as fuck brunette turned and lifted her sunglasses. Instead of focusing on Akino, her eyes met his.

With distaste.

What the hell?

Daniel slowly raised his brows. He couldn't remember the last time a woman had looked at him in such a way.

Oh wait, yes, he could. Never.

Her eyes moved from his to Akino and softened.

Before Daniel could stop himself, he sneered. Not that she noticed, because she was already greeting Akino warmly.

Standing head and shoulders taller, Daniel stared down at the stunning woman, taking in blue eyes that were much brighter than his own. She had naturally dark olive skin and was simply fucking gorgeous.

For the first time in his life, Daniel Dufort felt mesmerized by a woman.

Okay, yes, and aroused.

"Ms. Kāne, I'd like to introduce you to our chief executive, Mr. Dufort," Akino said.

Daniel smirked and plugged his hands into the pockets of his Ralph Lauren shorts. This was when she would show interest.

Money. Wealth. Power.

Women were drawn to it.

"Nice to meet you, Mr. Dufort," she said, completely void of any sincerity, and then reached out her hand. "Please, call me Harper."

Daniel glanced at her hand, then held her brilliant blue stare. Once of her eyes twitched as he knew it would, then he smiled and shook her hand.

All his smugness vanished as their skin touched. Heat poured through their connection as both their eyes widened.

Fuck.

She pulled her hand away, and they stood staring at each other in surprise.

Akino cleared his throat.

Say something. Say something.

"Ah, Ms. Kāne, I hope you're enjoying your stay at my hotel. You're Australian?" he asked.

Then she rolled her fucking eyes at him.

Cough, cough, cough. Akino began coughing beside him.

Daniel glared at him.

"No. I'm from New Zealand," Harper replied. "Different accent. Different country. Different island."

He knew where fucking New Zealand was. He didn't need her to give him a geography lesson. God, this woman was a snarky bitch.

Daniel had already decided he was going to fuck her, but now he had second thoughts. He'd just take her from behind, after she'd thoroughly sucked him off. Actually, no, he wanted to see those blazing blue eyes as she screamed his name.

He gave her his best scolding look, which seemed to have no effect. She glanced away with absolute disinterest.

"Ms. Kāne is the author I mentioned earlier. The one who will be working with the network this week."

Oh fucking great.

"Well," Daniel said, gritting his teeth. "I'm sure that will be a joyous occasion."

"Yes," she replied, dropping her glasses back over her eyes. "Mr. Dufort. I will see you in a few days. Akino, lovely to see you again. I am off to relax on the beach. Aloha."

And then she was gone.

Daniel watched her walk out of the large hotel entrance until she was out of sight. Slowly, his eyes moved back to Akino.

"I suspect she's jetlagged, sir," he said, smirking. "She seemed much friendlier last night."

He didn't need her friendly.

Just horizontal.

Or on her knees.

Harper Kāne was just the sexy distraction he was looking for.

CHAPTER FIVE

No, no, no, no, no.

Harper was almost stomping her way to the beach after leaving the hotel.

One glance at the tall Adonis of a man in the hotel—who just happened to own the damn thing—and she knew the universe was messing with her.

He'd all but fucked her with his eyes.

No men.

No damn men.

Even gorgeous men with broad shoulders stretched underneath a very nice white shirt, which likely covered a delicious set of golden abs she'd love to run her fingers over.

Even then.

Mostly.

And God, those eyes. Ice blue like a wild ocean.

When Daniel Dufort had taken her hand in his, it had caused a cocktail of reactions through her body. Embarrassingly so.

Worse, she had stared at his hand, thinking of what those fingers could do to her body.

How dare he?

How dare he tempt her with that dark wavy hair, or square, masculine jaw? His calculating gaze told her he was a powerful man who got what he wanted.

Once she'd got closer, Harper had recognized who he was. She'd researched the family and business for her novels years ago. Without his fancy business suits and rich women on his arm, he'd looked different. Unfortunately for her, the photos hadn't done him justice.

The truth was, Daniel Dufort was unreasonably gorgeous.

And knew it.

A man like him could have any woman he wanted. A man like him *had* every woman he wanted.

But he wouldn't have her.

She'd seen the desire in his eyes, and his frustration when she'd hidden her interest.

Harper may be young and inexperienced when it came to men, but she knew people. She studied people. It helped her as an author, and perhaps because of her distrust in men, she looked just that little bit closer.

No, Daniel Dufort would not have her, and she was going to keep a large distance to ensure she stuck to that promise.

Hopefully, she'd only have to see him during the one meeting they had together with *BookFlix* in a few days' time.

Why he was here, Harper had no idea. Daniel had stepped into the CEO role of Dufort Dynasty LLC two years ago, making him a very powerful and wealthy man. Surely, he had people to do this?

In fact, Harper was pretty sure his two brothers were more involved with the operational side of the business.

She flicked her towel out and lay it down on the sand.

"Trust me to catch the eye of a playboy billionaire," she muttered to herself. "Right out of a damn novel."

And he'd called her a damn Australian. How insulting. Perhaps she'd ask him where in Canada he grew up.

With an evil grin, she lay down and opened her steamy novel written by an author friend of hers.

Harper knew a man like Daniel wouldn't stay away once he had his eye on his prey, but she would do her best to avoid the hotel and him.

Four hours later, Harper was on her way back to the Dufort Waikiki.

She had hit the shops—and air conditioning— along Kalakaua Avenue, which was the main street in Waikiki. She loved being able to step from the beach into Michael Kors or even Prada, still wearing her bikini and jandals—or flip-flops, as they were called in America. Not that she could afford anything from Prada, but it was fun to pretend.

Maybe one day.

Swinging four shopping bags and sipping on a watermelon Jamba Juice, Harper walked into the hotel lobby.

She was already starting to feel the aloha vibes of the tropical islands relax and calm her. In a few days, the network would be here, and she was excited about where this would take her career.

She was already becoming well known, but this would take her books and her brand as an author to a global level.

Scary and exciting.

Harper dropped her shopping bags on her bed and pulled a mid-length white sundress over her bikini, then made her way to the rooftop bar for a late lunch.

"Aloha," the bartender said, greeting her.

"Aloha," she replied, sitting on a barstool.

"I'm Ted," said the tall blonde-haired man, who sounded and looked like he was from California. "What can I get you today?"

Harper took the bar menu from him and began to flick through it. She scanned the cocktail menu and selected a completely ridiculous looking one with all the pineapple and umbrellas. "I'll have a Hawaiian Village Sunset and chicken salad, please, Ted."

"Coming right up. Feel free to sit anywhere, and I'll find you," he smirked cheekily.

"Thank you," she blushed, swiveling off her stool. The Dufort Hotels were five-star luxury hotels. *BookFlix* was paying for her accommodation, otherwise she never would have been able to afford to stay there. With it came some lovely benefits such as a gym, the pool and all their restaurants.

Harper found a large, luxurious sun lounger with a side table and sat down with a long sigh. Ted was innocently flirting with her, but it had been a long time since a man made her feel pretty and desired.

These were the types of romances she wrote about. It was what she and millions of women dreamed of.

A shame that in reality most of them ended in heartbreak. Or was that her mother talking?

As if on cue, her phone beeped.

Harper. Reply to my texts and let me know you are safe.

Twenty-five. She was twenty-five damn years old, and her mother still treated her like she was fifteen. Even when she was engaged to David, nothing changed.

I'm alive and kicking in glorious Hawaii. I am not going to text you every day, Mother, so please let me have a holiday.

What if something happens to you? It's dangerous.

Harper sighed and threw her phone in her bag, then lay back on the lounger.

After a few minutes, a server delivered her cocktail and salad. Harper gave the young girl a smile and glanced at the bar where Ted was serving an older couple.

He caught her eye and winked.

She quickly glanced away.

That was the second time he'd made her blush, and while Ted was a good-looking guy, her body hadn't reacted in the same way it had when she met Daniel.

It was the difference between smoke and molten rock.

Another reason she would be wise to stay far, far away.

CHAPTER SIX

Daniel sat on the other side of the pool with his laptop open on the table. His dark sunglasses meant he couldn't see shit on the screen, but that wasn't what he was looking at.

He'd been watching Harper Kāne flirt with the bartender. Or rather, the bartender flirt with her.

And it had irked him.

She'd blushed and smiled at the young guy, then sashayed away. He hadn't detected any of the hostility she'd shown him.

Why the fuck not?

Daniel lifted his Mai Tai to his lips and finished his drink. As if by magic—and also because he owned the place—a server appeared asking if he wanted another one.

"Yes, thank you," he said, his eyes barely leaving Harper. As the server wandered off, Daniel called out, "Please send Ms. Kāne another drink. Anonymously."

"Yes, sir," she said, appearing to have no point of view on his request, but he knew it would be kitchen gossip in ten minutes.

He didn't care.

It wasn't the first time he'd been in one of his hotels and fucked a guest. From actors to musicians to politicians, he usually met one woman or another and ended up enjoying their…body.

Daniel was discrete but didn't hide who he was.

He wasn't married and enjoyed sex.

He didn't screw the crew. None of them did. It was company policy.

Harper wasn't the type of woman to usually grab his interest. She appeared to be in her mid-twenties and not terribly successful, despite the book deal with the network. As a businessman, he knew the opportunity, while probably exciting for Ms. Kāne, wasn't going to make her a rich woman.

Not that he chose woman based on their bank balance—that was irrelevant to him —he was simply surrounded by wealthy people because of the places he went and was invited to.

In some ways, it was easier. They understood the rules; If a man of his means was interested in a woman seriously, he would date her. He'd wine and dine her. Ask about what she wanted in life. Where she wanted to live. What kind of house she wanted. Did she want children? A holiday home in the Hamptons? He'd meet her parents, she'd meet his— well, maybe not his mother—and plans would be made.

Daniel never did any of those things.

So when he took them home, they knew the deal. It was pure sex. When he arranged a car before morning, they knew the deal. It was a one-time deal.

Would Harper?

Because he *was* going to fuck her.

And soon.

Daniel reclined in his seat and waited. He'd thought about her a lot during the day and his cock was eager to know her more. But he couldn't shake the way she'd looked at him with complete disinterest.

He, perhaps arrogantly, didn't buy it. Not that all women desired him—that simply wasn't true—but the fire in their touch had burned, telling a completely different story than the dismissive look in her eyes.

She'd tried to ignore it, but Daniel wasn't going to let that fly.

She was about to learn Daniel Dufort took what he wanted. And the more he watched her across from him, the more he wanted her.

Hell, he'd spent the day outside working, enjoying the tropical heat while he tried to distract himself from the blackmail and the sexy Kiwi woman who had turned and walked away from him.

He was failing at both.

Black Josh still hadn't responded, and the clock was ticking.

Daniel shivered.

Nadia Mackenzie was not a woman he wanted to spend his days or nights with.

Despite being a beautiful woman—tall, slim, with long dark hair to the middle of her back—and having an MBA from Brown, she was boring as fuck.

If this marriage did go ahead, and God he hoped it wouldn't, Daniel was going to demand a minimum term and set of requirements he suspected Nadia wouldn't be prepared for.

He'd make it as difficult as he could for them right to the very point that he signed his name on the marriage license.

Daniel was prepared to do it, if it meant saving Dufort Hotels, but it he'd have his own terms—terms his bride would unlikely enjoy.

There would be no sex, and Nadia would have to remain loyal to him for five years. If she was exposed as a cheater, the marriage would be void, along with the shares.

They could have the marriage, but he wasn't fucking her. Even Mackenzie wasn't sick enough to demand that of his daughter.

Was he?

Daniel felt his stomach turn. The asshole was capable of anything.

Across from him, the ridiculous-looking cocktail was delivered, and Harper looked up in surprise. He watched as she was informed the drink was an anonymous gift, and her mouth drop open. Then slam shut.

Oh, how Daniel wanted to slip inside that mouth of hers.

When the server disappeared, he watched Harper sit up and glance around.

The poolside bar was steady but not busy. It was the tail end of the lunch service, so people were heading to the beach, out on an afternoon tour, or to the shops. He knew this because it was his business to know the behaviors of his guests, and to capitalize on it.

By five o'clock, the bar would be packed as people lined up drinks to watch the sunset around six o'clock.

Harper's eyes darted from table to table, searching for her drink donor. She dashed past him, then those blue eyes quickly landed back on his and stopped.

Fire.

The now familiar heat flared through his body as she held his eyes from across the pool. His cock twitched in his shorts, as he imagined being deep inside her. Irritation crossed her face, but Daniel had enough experience to know she was simply trying to ignore her attraction to him.

He held back his smirk, instead lifting his glass in cheers, and taking a slow sip.

His eyes never leaving hers.

He'd been right. This was an author that needed a good fucking and Daniel was happy to volunteer a night of his time.

Soon she would be screaming his name, then after the meeting with *BookFlix* he'd never have to see her again.

CHAPTER SEVEN

How dare he?

Harper fought her manners, lifted her glass in thanks, and lay back down on the sun lounger. If Daniel Dufort thought she was going to walk across the bar and join him, he was mistaken.

Seriously, did she have a sign on her forehead saying, 'single and ready to have my heart broken again'?

No thanks.

She wasn't here for a holiday romance. Heck, she'd never even had a one-night stand.

Ever.

All she wanted to do was enjoy her holiday, max out her credit card, buy designer handbags and shoes, and drink cocktails under the tropical skies of Hawaii.

She was happy to make friends and enjoy a few drinks with people, or maybe even a friendly man, but it wouldn't go further than that.

Daniel Dufort was not that man. Accepting a drink with him was like lying down and opening your legs.

Which, yes, would likely be God damn amazing. But no.

God, she had to stop thinking about things like that. Heat flared between her legs, and she squirmed on the lounger.

Ugh. She had to stop. A man like him would notice those signs and jump to conclusions.

She sat up and glanced over.

He stared at her.

She flushed from head to toe.

God.

She had to speak to him and be very clear their relationship was strictly business. Then he'd move on to another victim.

Harper picked up her bag and cocktail and made her way around the pool to Daniel's table. She felt his eyes follow her the entire way.

Don't look at his chest. Or forearms. Or...just focus on his face.

"Aloha, Ms. Kāne." His voice was deep and gravelly, and her entire body turned to jelly.

God damn him.

She had to get out of here.

Harper lifted her cocktail. "I just wanted to say thank you before I head out."

As if studying his prey, Daniel's head slightly tilted, then he nodded.

Instead of leaving, she found herself staring at his muscular body. Every inch of him was perfect. He was the ultimate rich, powerful billionaire the gossip columns wrote about. From his Prada shoes, his big fancy watch—she had no idea about brands, but it likely cost more than her house—to his Tom Ford sunglasses.

Harper didn't care that she was wearing a fifty-dollar dress and her flip-flops had been a five-dollar bargain at The Warehouse—a big box retailer in New Zealand. She was more concerned that Daniel was looking at her like he wanted to lick her from head to toe.

And that she really wanted him to.

Her body tingled with need, and she blushed.

Daniel stood, and her eyes nervously followed his until they were looking down at her. Harper felt dwarfed by what had to be at least six foot three inches of controlled dominance. He stepped closer and placed a hand on the small of her back.

Oh God, more fire.

She swallowed.

"Before you do, please, join me for a moment," he said, or rather instructed, moving a chair out. "I thought we could get to know one another before our business meeting."

Don't sit down.

"Thank you," she said, sitting.

Fuck's sakes.

"I was going to ask if this was your first time visiting the islands, but your surname tells otherwise."

"My father was Hawaiian," Harper replied.

"Was? I'm sorry. You must miss him," Daniel said, and she was surprised how genuine it came across.

"Not really. He cheated on my mother and had another family here. We didn't know about them for several years." She shrugged. "So no."

If she'd been trying to shock Daniel Dufort, she'd just failed miserably. Instead of reacting, he just stared at her with no expression. Not even a blink.

Harper glanced away and took a sip of her drink. "Look, I—"

"Is that why your stories are based in Hawaii? Are you rewriting history?"

Harper's mouth dropped open. "My stories are not about my father. They're steamy romances about people who fall in love and live happily ever after. Escapism. Clearly fiction."

His lips twitched. "An unromantic romance author. How ironic."

She shrugged. All she wanted was for him to get the message she wouldn't be manipulated by his money, power, or charm.

To do that, she really needed to get away from him.

"Not all of us come from the perfect, privileged life," she said. His smug eyes turned dark. How predictable. Rich men rarely liked being put into boxes. "Tell me, Mr. Dufort, when will you be marrying your high school sweetheart or the perfect society girl?"

Instead of responding, he stared at her darkly until it became uncomfortable.

"Well, it looks like I'm not the only one capable of a *faux pas*, Ms. Kāne," he said, throwing back the rest of his drink.

A chill ran through her body as she watched him stand and collect his laptop and phone. Clearly, she had touched a raw nerve. She thought about apologizing but sat there frozen. Daniel leaned down, placing a hand on the back of her chair. Harper remained staring straight ahead, her back ramrod stiff.

"My mother was an alcoholic, and they divorced when I was thirteen. And there is no college sweetheart. Unlike you, I have no fantasies about marriage. I fuck. They leave. The end."

She turned as he stood and pulled his sunglasses down over his eyes.

"Enjoy the rest of your day, Ms. Kāne."

Shit.

CHAPTER EIGHT

Daniel gripped the metal bar and groaned as he pulled, feeling the extra weights he'd added this morning. The burn felt good. He did four more reps, then let it clang back into place and stood.

Why he let Harper Kāne get to him, he didn't know, but he had.

She wasn't the first person, nor would she be the last, to assume he'd lived a perfect life because of his wealth. But fuck, it was such an ignorant point of view.

What pissed him off even more was how her story about her father had momentarily moved him. What an asshole thing to do. Marry a woman, get her pregnant and then go start a new family.

Yeah, that guy had been an ass.

He imagined it would've been very upsetting and destabilizing as a child. It was unlikely she trusted men and explained her cynical view of love.

In that, they were matched.

So why then, when he was showing interest in her physically, was Harper not reciprocating? He could tell she was attracted to him.

His mind whirled.

It was unlikely she was a virgin.

Daniel pulled on his gloves and began punching the hanging bag.

Maybe it was best to sit this one out. She might not think she wanted love, but Daniel got the feeling Harper was trying to write her own love story.

His phone rang.

"Siri, answer call."

"Daniel," a deep voice said when the device answered.

Finally!

"Josh," Daniel replied. "I've got a job for you. You available?"

"Depends. What are we looking at?"

"US senator trying to blackmail me into marrying his daughter," he said, hardly believing he was saying those words out loud.

"Ah, that old nugget," Josh replied sarcastically. "Timing?"

Daniel pulled off his gloves, dropping them on the mat as he stepped closer to his phone. He leaned against the wall and crossed his arms, looking out over Waikiki. "We've got about three weeks, then they're threatening to go public with an announcement. If you're on board, I'll email you the details."

"Who are we looking at here?"

"Mackenzie."

Josh let out a growl. "That fucker."

The senator wasn't a well-liked or popular guy, and more than once, Daniel had wondered about his father's association with him.

"What does he want?"

"Shares. He's doctored some documents to extort my father. Further negotiations ended up with me being included. Apparently, the daughter has had her eye on my nether regions for some time. I guess they see this as a win-win."

And Daniel was going to make sure both of them fell from grace for this.

"How do you want to play this?"

"The figure they're asking for would destroy Dufort Dynasty, so we can't pay it out, nor can we prove the documents are forged. I need leverage. A man like Mackenzie will have left some crumbs to some illegal dealings somewhere. Find me the crumbs."

Josh cursed. "In three weeks? Fuck, Dufort."

"Sorry, man, next time I'm blackmailed I'll ask them to give us more of a heads up so you can plan better."

"Do that," Josh said, a grin in his voice. "Let me see where I land with this, and I'll come back to you in a few days. Assume the budget…"

"Whatever it takes."

"Gotcha."

A few hours later, Daniel was working at his desk when a video call came through. He clicked answer.

"You're alive." He smirked at Fletcher, who was sitting up in a private hospital bed.

"No, I'm calling from heaven to say you cannot have my Maserati."

Daniel grinned.

"How did it go?" he asked, referring to Fletcher's medical procedure. He'd had sudden and severe pain in his left knee over the past month. It turned out to be a ligament tear from running and required surgery.

"Good. The doc said I can go back to the gym and even run in about six weeks."

Of the three of them, Fletcher was the sportiest. Daniel was the broadest, preferring to lift weights and run two or three times a week.

Hunter had been into baseball when they were young. There was no time for team sports in their lives now, but one day he could imagine his brother coaching minor league if he had kids. That would entail him settling down, and he knew Hunter's sex life was more alternative than him or Fletch, but that was a whole different story.

Daniel wondered if either of them would have families. There was no shortage of women interested, but none of them had ever showed any interest in matrimony.

"Still unbelievable that you didn't feel the injury happen."

"Doc said it's common. I think I know when it happened, but there was no severe pain at the time, and I just carried on," Fletcher said, then began to smirk.

"If you are going to tell me it was some wild sexual act, please don't bother," Daniel said. "I've heard you're a missionary guy."

Fletcher laughed quietly and gave him the bird.

"Did you message Mom?" he asked, and Fletcher's smile faded.

It was difficult for all of them to be with her. While she was sober, Marie Dufort still hadn't forgiven their father and was full of anger about what could have been. It was the same conversation every time.

All of them had tried to help her in one way or another, but she wouldn't accept any of it.

"Yeah," he said. "I told her you were in Hawaii and…"

Together they both said, "*Your father and I honeymooned in Hawaii.*"

"Anyway, now that you are back in the world of the living, has Dad updated you on the Mackenzie situation?"

Fletcher shook his head.

"Of course not." He launched into the details of what had happened, leaving space for Fletcher to curse and shake his head.

"Hunter know?"

Daniel nodded. "Yeah, I updated him on the flight over. Sorry, bro, I just wanted you to focus on the operation."

"Appreciate it, but you didn't need to. I'm fine," he said. "But Jesus—Nadia fucking Mackenzie. Ouch."

Yeah, she was no Cinderella.

"So, what's the plan?"

Daniel wasn't telling anyone about *Black Hawke Security* so as not to incriminate others, so he focused on what they could do internally.

"Confidentially, prep Olivia on this engagement, becoming a possibility. Get her to sign a non-disclosure despite her employment contract. I want her thoughts on all scenarios. Set up a call if she wants to run through things. Keep Dad out of it," Daniel said, frowning. "We need this airtight from the board. The fewer people who know, the better."

"Are Brent and Tony aware of this new development?" Fletcher asked, referring to Dufort's corporate lawyer, and head of finance.

"No. All they know is Dad hasn't been able to find a copy of the document in his personal files.

"Because we all thought Dad would find the original agreement."

Daniel nodded. "Correct."

"Can't we get anyone to sign affidavits saying they witnessed seeing the original?" Fletcher asked.

"Against a US senator? It would get messy and public."

Fletcher signed. "Yeah, it would. God damn it."

"I'm not marrying her," Daniel said. "I have some other ideas on this, but for now, I need you and Olivia to be ready for the media if it comes to that."

Fletcher nodded.

"So, is everything going okay over there in paradise? You need anything from me? And have you met Harry yet?"

Daniel nodded and sat back in his chair, clasping his hands behind his head. "Yup. Good kid. He's smart and has everything handled. I met the author, too."

Why did he say that?

"Ah, what's her name? Hannah someone?"

"Harper. Harper Kāne."

"Okay." Fletcher stared at him, expecting him to add something more.

He pressed his lips together.

"Wait, is she hot?" Fletcher began tapping on his laptop. "Wow, fuck, she *is* hot. Damn."

Daniel felt his jaw tense at the thought of Fletcher being here with Harper instead of him.

Would she like him?

Fletcher attracted women just as much as he did. He had these bright green eyes they couldn't resist. So he'd been told. The more he imagined Fletcher with Harper, the tighter his jaw clenched.

"She'd eat you alive," Daniel growled.

"She'd be most fucking welcome to," Fletcher said, peering at the screen at her images.

"Would you stop that? She's a business partner. Kind of."

Fletcher's eyes returned to his and narrowed as he grinned. "You like her?"

Daniel frowned.

"Holy shit. Big brother finally has a crush. Fuck, I have to go ring Hunter."

Daniel held a hand up. "I *do not* have a damn crush. Don't—"

The call ended, and he slammed his laptop closed.

Jesus.

Daniel rolled his eyes. Anyone would think they were a bunch of teenage boys some days. Not executives running a multi-billion-dollar global enterprise.

Knock, knock, knock.

Daniel looked up. He made his way to the entrance and pulled the door open.

"Aloha, sir," the young Dufort staff member said. "I have been instructed to inform you we have a hurricane warning on the island for the next few days."

And?

He had watched the weather turning all day. Hurricanes were common in Hawaii, especially in February. Rarely did they eventuate into anything more than a bad storm despite the media dramatics.

"Thank you," he said and began to close the door.

"Sorry, sir, but Mr. Akino asked me to emphasize that this one is the real deal and likely to be a category five."

Daniel raised his brows.

"When will it arrive?"

"Overnight and into the early hours of the morning," the young man said. "We're boarding up and having supplies brought to your suite."

Okay, so a bit more serious than he'd assumed. Daniel knew all their staff were trained supplied with the necessary requirements for natural disasters or weather emergencies. As much as anyone could.

"We will notify guests if there's a need to move them into the corridors overnight. It's looking likely. Let me know if you want assistance moving your mattress."

"That's unnecessary," he said. "Is the PA system functioning?"

The man nodded. "Yes, sir, and the city is testing the sirens in about an hour."

Daniel pulled out his phone just as the Hawaiian Emergency notification sounded.

"Look after the guests. I can collect the supplies I need," he said when the blaring noise ended.

Like his brothers, his father had ensured they all worked in the Dufort hotels in several departments when they were younger. Daniel had changed sheets, washed dishes and—badly—checked guests in. Fletcher had been better face to face with people with all his natural charm.

"Thank you, sir," the guy replied, and they both knew Akino would never let that happen.

"Will *The Olive Tree* remain open?" he asked, referring to the bar in the center of the lower floor. It was away from windows, making it a safe spot for their guests.

"Yes, until one 1:00 a.m." Daniel nodded, and the man left.

They were lucky to have the internally located establishment. Every hotelier knew asking people to remain in their rooms for any length of time was unrealistic.

His mind flashed to Harper, and he wondered how she was responding to the news.

Not his problem.

Still, Daniel didn't like that she was on her own and possibly scared. However unlikely, given the woman was made of ice.

Daniel walked to the large windows and looked out over Waikiki Beach.

No, she was more like a snow lion, cold on the outside and warm on the inside.

Even though she'd pushed his buttons yesterday, he still intended to melt her ice façade and sink into all that heat. Deeply.

CHAPTER NINE

A loud blast shocked Harper out of her book coma, and she sat up, looking around.

What the fuck?

She heard a couple on the beach nearby talking about a hurricane approaching the islands. They were looking at their phones.

Oh.

She flopped back on the sand and lifted her book back into position. There were hurricanes in Hawaii every sixty seconds.

Not literally.

Granted, it *was* very windy today, and the beach was quiet, but there were still people swimming and sunbathing.

Harper let her mind dissolve away as she headed back to her vampire novel and all its sexiness. The hero was about to realize the girl was his fated mate. It was a steamy, big romantic moment.

Twenty minutes later, she was finding it hard to hold the pages and finally admitted defeat. She noticed people had begun to frantically pack up and began to put her own belongings in her beach bag.

Maybe this was more serious than she realized?

"Excuse me, ma'am, you need to return to your hotel," a surf lifeguard advised her. "Category five."

He continued on his way to the next group on the beach as Harper looked down at her phone and saw the emergency messages from the state of Hawaii.

Crap.

Just her damn luck.

The wind whipped around her and the farther up from the beach she got, the worse it felt. Glancing up, she saw the clouds were darkening, despite the still warm temperature, and felt fine raindrops on her arms.

Harper picked up speed and stood, tapping her feet as she waited to cross the street.

On each corner in Waikiki there were *ABC* stores which sold every kind of convenience you could imagine, from clothes, gifts, alcohol, snacks, fruit, water, to suntan oil, and so on.

Harper headed toward the closest one and found it packed with people stocking up on supplies. She pushed her way through and found a lot of bare shelves, so she began throwing things into a basket.

She hated panic shopping, but her father had told her many times that islands like Hawaii were only stocked with seven days' worth of food. If ships and planes couldn't access them for any reason, food would quickly run out.

Well, except pineapples and macadamia nuts. Both of which grew in abundance on the islands.

Harper grabbed a bottle of vodka, potato chips, as many bottles of water as she could carry, and chocolate.

"Mahalo," she said, thanking the server and lifted the heavy bags. As soon as she stepped outside, the wind blasted her, and for the first time in her life, Harper wondered if she could be blown off her feet by nature.

It was impossible to run with all her bags, so she walked fast, keeping her head down, and finally arrived back at the hotel. Except the doors were locked.

"Shit."

"This way, ma'am," a man called farther down the drive as he came running out of a side door. He took a couple of her bags and helped her inside.

Harper dropped her things to the floor as the door closed behind her and let out a sigh. She wiped her wet hair off her face.

Outside, the storm continued to roar while Dufort staff raced around, clearly preparing for the hours ahead of them.

"Mahalo," she said, thanking the man.

He led her farther into the hotel and dropped her bags onto one of the guest sofas in the lobby.

"What do we need to do?" she asked, feeling a little nervous. She may not have ever lived in Hawaii, but she'd grown up hearing stories from her father. While it was rare for a big one to hit, when they did, it could be very serious.

Plus, as a New Zealander, they were surrounded by Pacific Islands who regularly got hit by mother nature. She was well aware of its destructive abilities.

"It would be best if you returned to your room and packed up your belongings. Put them in the bathroom," he said. "If we think it's necessary, you may be instructed to move to the hallways for the night."

"To sleep?" she asked, her eyes wide.

The man nodded.

Suddenly, a shiver ran down her spine, setting her senses on fire.

"I'll take Ms. Kāne from here. Thank you, Kanoa," Daniel said, and the man smiled and left. Daniel picked up the ABC bags and gave her a penetrating glance. "Are you all right?"

Harper glanced down at her bedraggled look. Her wet hair was plastered to the side of her face and if she hadn't been wearing a navy bikini under her sundress, things would have been quite embarrassing.

She pushed her wet hair off her face and could tell by his slight grin it had only made things worse.

"I'm, yes, I'm okay, thank you," she said, then reached for the bags. "I can take those."

Daniel ignored her and began walking away. Harper picked the other bags up and hurried after him. When she reached the wall of lifts to stand next to him, he'd already pressed the button.

"I can take them," she said, more quietly.

He glanced down at her and shook his head. "Accept some help, Harper. It won't kill you."

She chewed her lip and stepped inside the lift as the door opened. Daniel stepped in and sucked up all the air, making it difficult for her to breathe.

They'd been in close proximity before, but now they were on their own, and in the small space, he seemed much bigger.

Daniel pressed number thirty-five on the panel and her eyes narrowed. How did he know what floor she was staying on? He may own the hotel, but that was a little creepy.

"Not a fan of storms?" he asked, not looking at her.

"Is anyone?"

Daniel shrugged. "Sure. There are storm chasers."

She glanced up at him. "There are?"

He nodded and his eyes moved to look at her. They were full of humor.

"Are you one of them?" she asked, curious.

The door opened, and they walked down the hallway. When they reached her room, she pulled out her card and Daniel took it from her.

Swipe.

The door beeped, and he opened the door, allowing her to enter first. She moved past him, feeling his body heat as she did, and placed the bags on the hotel room dining table.

Daniel did the same and stood looking around her room, frowning. "We should get you an upgraded suite."

First, it wasn't a suite—it was a standard room. *BookFlix* had paid for her flights and accommodations, and it was sufficient.

"This is fine," she replied, feeling a little embarrassed. "It's all I need."

And all I can afford, but you wouldn't understand that.

"So are you? A storm chaser?" She asked again.

Suddenly she found herself standing way too close to him, her hair dripping down her neck.

Daniel's eyes traced the water past her collarbone, down to her breasts, and she felt her face flush. Then those eyes darted back to hers.

"No. I dance with danger in other ways," he said. "Apparently."

Dammit, she did not want to be attracted to this man, and yet she felt her core clench and her nipples harden. She bit her lip, trying to hide her reaction, and when she looked at Daniel, she expected a smug grin, but instead there was fire in his eyes.

Oh, God.

Harper drew in a long, slow, rattly breath and licked her lips.

Don't lick your lips, dammit.

Daniel's eyes followed the movement, but the wind rattling wildly against the window broke the spell.

Harper turned sharply.

Daniel placed his hand on her arm, and she jumped a little. "Get changed and meet me down in *The Olive Tree*. You'll feel safer down there."

Harper's brows furrowed. This was a bad idea.

"It's going to be a long night, Harper, and I want to know you're okay and not here alone freaking out."

"Why do you care?" she asked.

His crystal blue eyes narrowed. "I don't know. It's a good fucking question."

Harper stared back at him, unsure of what to do. If she said no, Daniel would find some other female to while away the hours of this storm. Why did he want her?

"It's just a drink or two. In public." He said as he walked to the door. "I won't bite. I'll be there until 10:00 p.m."

Then he was gone.

Harper let out a long breath and slumped on the bed. If she went, and despite what he'd said, she knew a man like him would have expectations.

The only reason she was even contemplating going was because of the damn storm, and she also felt terrible about the way they'd ended things up at *Altitude*.

Harper owed him an apology, so clearing the air before they had to conduct business together in a few days was a smart move. This meeting with *BookFlix* was important to her. She'd join him for a drink and then return to her room.

If Daniel thought he was going to have *his* way with her, he would be disappointed.

She'd need to keep her wits about her, though. Every time he was near, her body burst into flames and her brain malfunctioned. She'd just keep her distance and stick to one drink.

Harper quickly showered, dressed in a black sundress with spaghetti straps, and packed up her belongings as she'd been instructed. Outside, the hurricane roared and slammed against the surrounding buildings violently.

She carried her luggage into the bathroom and took another look in the mirror.

What would she have to talk to a billionaire from New York about? She knew nothing about him aside from what was online. Which was no doubt lacking in any truth.

If she tried hard to forget he was a broody, sexy billionaire, perhaps she might relax and enjoy herself. After all, they were just riding out the storm together.

Not riding…each other.

Christ.

Perhaps it was better if she just drank and let him do the talking.

CHAPTER TEN

The Olive Tree was bustling with guests and nervous tension.

The Dufort staff were trained to ensure there was no heavy drinking on a night like this. While it was good for the cash register, it could mean trouble if a genuine emergency happened. The bartender had explicit instructions to count drinks and monitor customer behaviors. It was one reason Daniel had decided to hang out in the bar—not that he was needed. He knew Akino and his team had things covered.

The other reason was Harper. Who had not yet shown, but Daniel was confident she would.

Arrogantly.

He'd seen the quake in her lips as he'd stepped near. He'd watched her pupils dilate. Damn, he'd fought hard to stop himself from planting his lips on hers in that moment.

Water had been dripping down her neck and between her breasts, and his cock had stood straight up. Then, when he'd seen her nipples harden, the need to have her had been damn near overwhelming.

Harper needed to be fucked.

By him.

Hell, he needed to fuck her.

That wasn't why he'd invited Harper down for a drink, though. He could have taken her right there in the room and she would have let him. Instead, he had a genuine concern that had been nagging at him since he'd heard about the hurricane. Then, when he'd seen her in the lobby, his feet had just begun walking toward her. For some reason, he needed to ensure she was safe.

More than safe.

He wanted her upgraded and in a nice room.

Near him. Since when did he want a woman near him? Daniel lifted his whisky and tossed it back.

Speaking of…he opened his phone and checked to see if his lawyer had emailed the draft prenup through.

Nothing.

Jesus, what was the guy doing?

He fired off a quick follow up.

When he looked up, he stilled. Harper stood in the entrance of *The Olive Tree* in a figure-hugging black sundress, her long dark waves flowing around her shoulders. She was looking for him, but Daniel didn't wave out. He wanted to freeze frame the image of her.

She was fucking gorgeous.

"*Wow,*" the bartender said under his breath and Daniel glared at him. The guy caught his look and suddenly got busy wiping the bar.

When he turned back, Harper was making her way over to him. Daniel slid off the barstool and held her stare until they were standing in front of each other.

"Hi," she said quietly.

There was a sense of vulnerability about her, which had Daniel tilting his head. He had a feeling Harper didn't show it often and yet here it was on show for him.

She shouldn't—he was a predator.

He was going to eat her alive, from the top of her head to the tips of her toes. And yet the blush on her cheeks did something to him. His chest warmed, and he felt this need to pull her against him.

Instead, Daniel leaned in and kissed the sensitive spot along her jawline, right near her ear. He heard her small intake of breath, and his body roared.

"Thank you for joining me." He pulled out the stool and guided her onto it only so he could touch her.

Harper smiled in thanks and turned to the bartender. "A Sauvignon Blanc, please. Something from New Zealand. The Marlborough region preferably."

Daniel grinned.

"What?"

"I'm impressed. A woman who knows exactly what she wants instead of waiting for a man to order for her."

Harper put her small purse on the bar and frowned. "Why would I let a man order my drink?"

Women in his world did. Without hesitation. As if the minor act of him purchasing a twenty-dollar glass of wine for them meant a proposal was imminent.

Daniel was impressed with Harper's show of independence. And yet this unreasonable and uncharacteristic need to take care of her kept growing within him.

He couldn't ignore it, and if she resisted him, he'd just need to persuade her. Daniel was a man of power and got what he wanted.

He wanted to look after this woman.

He needed her to know she was safe.

With him.

"Aloha, Mr. Dufort, Ms. Kāne," Akino said, joining them. He looked unusually disheveled, which was understandable given the weather emergency.

He handed Daniel a hotel room card and nodded. "It's all sorted. I'll let you…" he nodded at Harper, "you know, as I've got to get back to the kitchen."

"Thank you, Akino," Daniel said. "Please let me know if I can be of any help."

"Thank you, sir, but we're fine. The team will distribute the dinner packs within the hour."

Daniel nodded and watched Akino race off.

"Dinner packs?" Harper asked.

Daniel lifted his fresh glass of whisky and nodded. "Yes, the kitchen closes for safety reasons during such an event, but the teams put together meal packs and distribute them to guests."

Harper nodded. "That's nice."

"We don't want our guests starving." He smirked.

"I guess not." She grinned. "What's in them?"

"No idea."

Harper let out a loud laugh, and he couldn't stop the smile from forming on his face.

My God. Her laughter lit up the whole God damn room. She was beautiful.

"I guess it's not exactly the CEO's job to know that stuff."

He grinned and studied the humor swirling in her eyes, his own going dark with need.

Harper lifted her glass of wine to her lips, and her smile faded as the heat between them intensified. It was more than heat—it was a connection. Daniel wanted to make her laugh again. He wanted to know what made her happy, sad, angry.

"I'm sorry," she blurted.

"For what?" He frowned.

"What I said yesterday. You're not—"

"Living an idyllic life?" he asked, harsher than he meant to. "Look, don't sweat it. It's a common assumption."

She gave him a small nod.

"Apology accepted. I shouldn't have reacted. I just have some stuff going on."

Stop talking, Daniel.

"Oh?"

And that's why he needed to stop talking. Harper was a bright woman. She wasn't going to miss a beat.

"Work stuff."

"So not a childhood sweetheart thing?" she asked, studying him.

"Are you asking if I'm single, Harper?" he asked, studying her back. "Because we both know I'm not married, and I'm wondering what we're doing here if you think I have a woman at home warming my bed."

She held his stare, fire brewing in her eyes. Then she blinked, put her wine down and folded her hands in her lap.

"I'm having a drink with a business associate who was kind enough to ask about my welfare during a hurricane."

No, she fucking wasn't.

Daniel lifted his whisky and tipped it heavily while deciding how to play this.

"And you?" he asked, ignoring her comment. "Do you have a husband or man warming your bed back home in New Zealand, Harper?"

He watched her blush cover her cheeks and down to her plump decolletage and wondered for a moment if she did.

"No."

"Well, then," he said, leaning his elbow on the bar and smiling.

"Well then, what? What does that mean?" she asked defensively and damn, he loved watching her unravel. Daniel knew then and there she would be a dynamite in bed.

"Well then, I guess we can relax and enjoy ourselves this evening," he said, sliding the room card across the bar toward her. "I forgot. This is for you."

Harper's eyes widened as she looked at it and then up at him. "Daniel. That's highly inappropriate."

He smirked. He knew what she was thinking and was enjoying her discomfort so much he left it a long moment before he corrected her.

Daniel sat back. "I am a confident man, Harper. If I wanted to have you in my room, I wouldn't slip you a room card. I would walk you up there myself." She started to respond, but he kept talking. "I had you upgraded. There are no strings attached."

Unless you want there to be.

He fully intended to have her in his bed, but for the first time in his life, he was enjoying the hunt to make it happen.

She picked up the card and turned it over multiple times. "I told you my room was fine. It's absolutely fine. Truly, this wasn't necessary."

It was.

For reasons he couldn't explain, he wanted Harper to enjoy the luxury he could provide. She was currently in their most basic room, and it wasn't right. Harper Kāne deserved far better.

Daniel shrugged and threw the rest of his whisky back, indicating to the bartender for another. The guy couldn't keep his eyes off her—nor could a handful of men around them. It was another reason Daniel was pleased he had upgraded her. If they had to sleep in the hallways tonight, there was no way he was going to leave her unprotected.

Harper didn't know it yet, but she had the second penthouse on the same floor as him.

"It's higher, but once this storm passes, I'm sure you'll enjoy the amenities," he said. "Your things have been moved."

Her mouth parted, and there was something about her lips, as her tongue danced over them, which drew him like a moth to a flame. He felt his pants tighten as their eyes met, then desire roared through him.

Was she aware of the way she looked at him?

"Harper…"

"Thank you," she said quickly, and looked away.

Fuck.

She was going to kill him with this hot and cold bullshit. How long would she deny her desire for him?

The problem was, Harper wasn't the kind of woman who wanted him for his power or his money. She was the kind of girl who wanted a husband and a picket fence. The exact opposite of what he could offer.

Everything about this was a bad idea.

She knew it. He knew it.

Yet here he was, not walking away, and he didn't know why.

"You're welcome." he replied.

"So what's it like living in Manhattan?" she asked, swirling her wine around in her glass.

Daniel tilted his head and pressed his lips together. He'd lived in New York City all his life. Sure, his address had improved over the years as Dufort Hotels began to grow, and then, as a young adult, he had quickly become wealthy in his own right.

Daniel had shares in many other enterprises, and though he didn't have much time to focus on them himself, he hired experts to grow his money.

Another reason his lawyer would be busy right now, ensuring everything he owned was rock solid and protected in his trust. Because of his role as CEO, all his financial assets were in public record.

Mostly.

"Cold right now," Daniel replied, noticing Harper had unconsciously moved closer to him, their legs touching. "Busy. Noisy. Vibrant. Have you visited?"

She shook her head.

He studied her. "You'd hate it."

"Why? How can you say that when you barely know me?" she asked, laughing at him.

"I know people," he replied.

People like Harper got eaten alive in New York City. She was too nice. Not that he thought she wasn't smart—she most definitely was—but there was a purity about her that would be lost after trying to survive in the big apple. It ate people and spat them out. "Tell me about New Zealand."

She let him get away with his comment and described her country. "It's a lot like Hawaii. It's a set of islands that's isolated from most of the world. It's very green. We have some big cities, and the people are pretty friendly, but without the aloha spirit, unfortunately."

Given her connection to Hawaii, it shouldn't have surprised Daniel that Harper understood that aloha was more than just a greeting. It was an essence, or energy, which existed on the islands and within the culture of the people.

He wondered why it had taken him so long to return to Hawaii. Until he'd become CEO, he had regularly traveled the world visiting London, LA, Sydney, Paris, Rome, and many of their other hotels.

Hawaii had always been his favorite.

Daniel watched Harper tapping her foot lightly to the music and take in her surroundings. From time to time, she pulled her hair over one shoulder and flicked it back and forth. She had no idea the impact she was having on him and many of the men nearby.

But it was only him she was giving little smiles to and blushing. Whether she was aware of it or not.

And fucking hell, he felt like superman.

From the moment they'd met, she had been so defensive, and now she had her walls down, relaxed. Still, he wondered what might make a woman be like that.

He suspected he knew.

It wasn't just her father who had deserted her. A man she loved had. At a guess fairly recently. Harper was a young woman. Daniel put her somewhere in her mid-twenties. If she had been with her boyfriend for a few years, it meant she hadn't had much experience with men.

He wasn't saying she was a virgin, not at all. She was well aware of the sexual energy between them, and he could see in her eyes she knew what to do with it. Harper was simply fighting it.

Now he knew why. Or strongly suspected, but he was pretty confident he was right.

She might have been a woman he wanted to fuck, but she wasn't someone you fucked and left.

And that was a problem.

CHAPTER ELEVEN

Harper placed her wineglass on the bar and turned to get the barman's attention, which wasn't hard. The man had been ogling her since she'd arrived.

She wanted to warn him it was a career-limiting move, given she was technically on a date with Daniel Dufort.

Technically.

She got the sense Daniel didn't share his toys.

And she was a toy to him.

Daniel placed his hand on her wrist, sending shockwaves through her body. Her eyes moved to his.

"What do you want? I'll order it," he said with authority, the silvery blue of his eyes swirling as they ran over her face.

"Just water, please. I've had enough wine."

He ordered them two waters while she took in his profile. Perfectly firm jaw, long eyelashes, and dark stubble made him look even more damn sexy than he did during the day.

He turned back to her, and they sat without speaking, gazing at each other. Candlelight danced across their faces while the world seemed to barely exist outside of their bubble.

She desperately wanted Daniel to touch her, and the need was becoming unbearable. At the same time, she was telling herself to run as far away as possible before she succumbed to his spell.

The longer she stayed, the more intense it felt.

Their water arrived, and she glanced away, taking a long drink. Daniel did the same as the tension between them swirled around them.

She had to leave. If she looked at him one more time, he was either going to kiss her, or she was going to throw herself at him.

Then her stomach made an embarrassing noise.

"Hungry?" he asked, smirking

"Apparently." She blushed and let out a small giggle. It was a sign to leave. Tossing back her drink, she dropped it on the bar and stood. "Thank you for your company tonight. I'm going to see if one of those meal packs has arrived in my new room."

A roar sounded outside, and she let out a little gasp. Daniel stiffened and placed his water on the bar firmly. "Wait, Harper."

From the bar she could see the wind slashing the windows and large palm trees swaying beside the streetlights. Her eyes darted to Daniel. "Do you think we'll be sleeping in the hallways?"

Daniel stood and reached for his phone, typing a text. "Let me find out."

As he typed, they walked out of the bar and his hand landed on the small of her back. Harper had clearly drunk enough wine to give her the courage to lean into him, and she did. And he felt warm and delicious.

They stopped just outside the entrance to *The Olive Tree*, where Daniel positioned himself close. His towering height and size gave her a sense of security she welcomed.

"Oh!" she said, turning suddenly into his body and finding his glittering eyes closer than she'd expected. Her hand flew to her chest like she was some maiden from another time. One day she'd laugh at herself, but right now she was all kinds of flustered by this powerful man. "I don't know what floor I'm on or the room number."

Daniel grinned. "Follow me, gorgeous."

Gorgeous? A million butterflies took flight inside her stomach.

No, no, no.

She couldn't fall for this guy. Billionaires from New York didn't fall in love with Kiwi girls. Harper closed her eyes and shook her head. "No, it's fine. Just tell me and I can find my way. Can't be that hard, can it?"

"Humor me, Harper. Let a man walk you home after buying you drinks," he said, glancing down at her with a frown.

"Sorry. I'm not very experienced with this dating stuff," she said and wished she could zip her lips closed.

Damn wine.

"You don't date?"

She shook her head.

"Ever?"

Harper let out a sigh. "My fiancé of five years left me three months ago. I dated a few guys when I was a teenager, but otherwise, no."

She felt her cheeks blush with embarrassment.

"A bit different from the usual woman you take out for a drink, I bet."

She risked a glance up at the man standing far too closely. He looked down at her and nodded. "Very."

Harper bit the side of her cheek, feeling like a fool. While she'd been trying to keep away from this man, she knew she wanted him. Foolishly, she had thought he would want her too.

How silly of her.

Daniel Dufort had experienced beautiful women in his life, who were no doubt fabulous dates. Afterwards, he'd go home with them and have wild sex she could only dream of.

Perhaps with two women.

Her eyes widened.

God, she was so inexperienced. She'd wanted to try different things, but David had told her to stop reading her book porn.

"It doesn't make them more attractive," Daniel said, turning to face her.

"It?"

His hand lifted to her cheek. "The women back home. You're an extremely beautiful and sexy woman, Harper."

She swallowed.

"Your ex. He was a fool to leave you," he added, his eyes dark as he stared at her lips like his life depended on it.

She blinked.

Was he going to kiss her?

She licked her lips before she knew what she was doing, and he groaned.

"If you do that again, Harper, I know you have enough experience to understand what I'm going to do next."

She swallowed and nodded.

Please do it.

"Is that a yes?" he asked, his eyes darting from her lips to her eyes, looking for her answer.

Her mouth parted to answer, and the doors dinged open. Harper looked behind him into the hallway, and Daniel tightened his grip on her face.

"Answer the question," he demanded, his other hand pressing the button to hold the lift doors open. And then he was taking a step closer, pressing her against the glass wall.

A small noise escaped her.

"I need you to say yes." His mouth was mere inches from hers.

Oh, God

If she did this, she knew what would happen. Her brain told her to say no. Her body was screaming yes.

She needed this. She needed to be desired and have wild, crazy sex with completely the wrong man.

Just once.

To be free of trying to get it right for once.

If she knew this wasn't going to be more than just sex, she could do this. Right?

No expectations. Just sex, and that was it.

Totally.

"Yes," she whispered, as Daniel slammed his mouth down on hers.

He took her. He stole from her. He completely owned her mouth, stealing all the oxygen from her lungs. Desire and heat unlike anything she'd felt filled every cell of her body, setting her on fire.

Daniel groaned and pulled her up against his body and she felt his desire for her against her stomach. Like him, it was big, and moisture pooled in her panties.

He crushed her to the wall as he devoured her mouth, while her hands gripped his shoulders, feeling his solid muscle. She gave over to him, feeling more feminine than she'd ever felt in her life.

This man was taking her very essence in just one damn kiss.

Then it ended, and they stood there panting, their bodies still crushed together.

"Jesus, Harper," Daniel said, his thumb rubbing over her lip. He was frowning at her. "Tell me you're wet right now."

"Very." she replied breathlessly.

"I'm going to take care of that," he said, and guided her out of the lift.

Though she was in a daze, she noticed something odd about this floor. There were no doors. "Are you sure we are on the right floor?" Then she shook her head. Daniel owned the damn hotel. "No offense."

"I'm sure," he said, letting out a small laugh.

He swiped her card, and the door swung open.

Harper stepped inside and froze.

"Daniel. What did you do?"

CHAPTER TWELVE

Yes, it's the penthouse, Harper. Quickly look around, get excited, and then let's get your damn clothes off.

God, he needed to fuck her, and fast.

That kiss.

Fucking hell.

Feeling her body against his, he'd nearly lost his damn mind. His cock was taking the driver's seat, and he was struggling to maintain control.

"I upgraded you." Outside, the hurricane winds slammed against the floor-to-ceiling glass, which ran the length of the suite, and lightning flashed in the sky.

Daniel quickly closed the curtains and turned on a few lights. They flickered but remained on. He hadn't heard from Akino yet, but Daniel strongly suspected tonight they would, in fact, be sleeping in the hall. This was as bad a hurricane as he'd ever seen.

Harper spotted her suitcases in the bathroom entrance and walked over to them, running her fingers across the top of them.

"This is too much, Daniel," Harper said, looking up at him.

"Enough," he said, walking over to her and taking her chin in his hand. "I wanted you to have a nice room. I look after…"

He was going to say *my own,* but what the hell?

"I'm next door in the other penthouse suite."

Her eyes flew open. "This is the penthouse floor?"

"Yes." He nodded. "Look, Harper, if we are sleeping in the hallways tonight, I'm not having you out there on your own unprotected."

She swallowed and nodded.

"Sorry. No one has ever done something like this for me before," she said, and looked around at the luxury that came with one of Waikiki's most glamourous hotel rooms.

Daniel grit his teeth. Why hadn't they? If she was his, he'd give her fucking everything.

His? What the hell?

Who was he to talk? He fucked women and left them. He was going to do the same to Harper, and they both knew it.

He spotted a package on the table and nodded to it. "Your meal package."

Harper smiled and opened the box. He heard mumbling, then she lifted her head and frowned. In her hand was a sandwich, which she waved at him like an angry Italian grandmother. "This. No. This is just not acceptable."

Daniel nearly laughed. "You don't like sandwiches?"

"Gluten, Daniel. Damn gluten," she growled.

Ah.

"You're coeliac?" he asked, wondering why his team hadn't accounted for food allergies.

"Intolerant. But that's not the point." She sighed, pulling out muesli bars, muffins, and a slice of cake—all of which contained flour. "Sorry, it's just a pet peeve."

Finally, she pulled out an apple and shrugged.

Before she could bite into it, he stopped her. "You're right. Put that down. An apple isn't a meal—not after all that wine. Come with me."

Daniel couldn't believe he was doing this, especially when all he wanted to do was strip her naked and sink deep inside her, but here he was, dragging Harper through the hotel to the kitchen. Only a skeleton staff was left. A few of them looked at him curiously, not sure who he was.

"Mr. Dufort is there something I can get for you?" one chef said, coming out of one of the large coolers.

His identity was now out in the open, the staff continued what they were doing.

"Ms. Kāne and I wish to make ourselves a gluten-free meal. There's no need to trouble yourself. We will be in and out," Daniel said with authority. He knew what chefs were like. Like the captain of a ship, they were dominant over their domain.

But this was his hotel, and he wanted to make Harper a meal. His expression gave no space for negotiation or denial. He watched as the chef wisely nodded and left them to it.

"Are you sure this is okay?" Harper asked as he led her into one of the coolers, making sure to prop the door open, and waved out his hand.

"Eat the entire place if you want to," he said, taking her chin and planting a kiss on her lips briefly. He had to taste her again soon. "Because if I need to remind you, this is *my* hotel."

They were both frozen by the physical connection and leaned into each other.

"Go, eat," he whispered against her lips

Harper nodded. She stepped away and began digging through containers. Daniel grabbed a bunch of grapes, cheeses, and some rice crackers.

"Wow, this is incredible," she said. "I wish I had a chef. Some women want a cleaner, but if I could, I'd have someone cook for me every day."

They laid out their food on a large platter as they talked.

"Really? You don't cook?"

Harper shrugged. "I do, but now that it's just me, the incentive is low and because I spend a lot of time writing, cooking is just a pain."

He had a housekeeper who maintained his home, did his shopping, and made meals. If he didn't arrive home in time to eat it when it was freshly made, it was in the oven or fridge, with instructions on how to heat it up.

Delicious gourmet meals. Every damn day.

Harper would be in heaven.

And of course, each meal was designed especially for him by his nutritionist and trainer, so he stayed in optimal shape.

He paid them to do all the thinking and doing so he could reap the benefits as he spent his days running a multi-billion-dollar business.

Daniel wasn't going to tell Harper any of that. It would only create a divide between them Daniel didn't want to exist. They pulled up a couple of stools hidden under a bench and began nibbling on their put together meal. He opened a bottle of water for Harper and handed it to her.

"Thank you."

As she placed a grape in her mouth and her tongue wrapped around it, his cock hardened. Then the weirdest thing happened. While he wanted nothing more than to bend her over and pull her panties off, letting his tongue dive into her wetness, Daniel suddenly felt an overwhelming need to know her more.

He wanted to know what else she liked and disliked, and how he could give her all those things and watch her face light up again?

Daniel stared at the plate of food in front of him. He didn't know where these thoughts were coming from. Was it because she'd been so disinterested in him, and he was having to put in some effort to have her?

He knew he wasn't Harper's type. It was one thing to be a rich asshole and think all women wanted you—and often they did for just one night, just as he did—but not many women could handle his life and all it entailed. Money and luxury, sure. But he worked long hours. He was never going to marry or have children.

She wasn't what he wanted, and it didn't sit well in his chest.

Why?

Sexually, they both wanted each other. That was all this was.

Suddenly the PA system crackled, and all guests were advised they were moving out into the hallways for their safety. Their belongings, especially valuables, should be moved inside the bathrooms and not taken out into the hallways with them.

Then a reminder to take their swipe keys.

Yeah, that was always a logistical nightmare after these things.

Harper's eyes darted to his in concern.

"It's okay," he said, tucking her hair behind her ear. "Let's go back and set up."

Ten minutes later, Daniel dragged Harper's mattress out of her bedroom and into the hallway. They were heavy fuckers, but it was better than sleeping on the floor.

"I hate this," she said, wrapping her arms around her middle.

"Trust me, if those windows blow, we'll both be covered in glass. So let's hightail it, okay?" he said just as the wind howled, making Harper jump.

"Jesus," she said and ran to the door.

"Hold it open. I'm coming through." Daniel gripped the mattress and pulled with all his strength, grateful for his weight training. In one effort, aside from navigating it through the doorway, it fell to the floor in a bang.

Harper raced inside and dragged the covers and pillows out, then the door closed behind them. When they had set up the bed against the far corner of the hallway, they both flopped down on it, breathing hard.

After a few minutes, she turned to him in question.

"Are you going to…" her eyes darted to the end of the hall, and he frowned.

"You want me to leave?" Daniel asked in disbelief. The building swayed and creaked, and Harper jumped into his arms.

Much better.

"No. Will you stay with me tonight?" she asked, just as the lights flickered off and they were plunged into complete darkness. "Oh, my God!"

"Give it a second," he said, rubbing her back. Daniel knew there would be hundreds of scared guests right now, but in five, four, three, two, one…and the lights flickered back on as the generator kicked in.

"Oh, thank God," she said, burying her face in his chest.

"You're safe, Harper. Nothing is going to bring this building down." Well, maybe an earthquake, but there was no point scaring her with those kinds of facts. "I'm going to turn off the lights at this end so we can try to sleep."

He climbed off the mattress and found the switch. The lights at the other end were still bright and disturbing, but it offered some relief.

"I doubt I'll sleep," Harper said as Daniel pulled his wallet and phone out of his pockets and kicked off his shoes.

Beside him, Harper removed her sandals and bra.

They lay down, and Daniel placed his arm under her head. It felt strangely comfortable. Strange in that he never simply lay down with a woman and cuddled or chat, but here he was.

The lust hadn't disappeared, but the odd circumstances they found themselves in had pushed pause on things for a bit.

Plus, since that moment in the kitchen, Daniel had felt different.

"Hi," Harper said, turning to him shyly.

He ran his hand over her face. "Just so you know, this isn't a normal date."

She let out a small giggle and he grinned.

"I had fun tonight," he said, surprising himself.

"I bet I know your favorite part."

"I bet you don't," he said, feeling the now familiar desire for her begin to stir. His eyes traced every inch of her face and its perfection. She was simply beautiful. Especially the three nearly invisible but matching freckles on her cheeks.

"I meant our meal in the kitchen," Harper said, her eyes sparkling. Daniel lifted on one arm and stared down at her. Suddenly, she turned into the vulnerable and feminine Goddess he'd kissed.

"No, you didn't," he said, his lips close to hers.

Her hand reached up, and she ran her fingers through his hair. Daniel closed his eyes, feeling her touch through his whole body.

He wanted her so badly now, but couldn't risk fucking her out here. If one of his staff stepped out of the lifts, they would see them. There was no way he'd let anyone see her naked. Would he have given any other woman in the past the same respect? He'd like to think so, but his need to fuck them would've likely dominated all else.

Hell yes, he wanted to fuck Harper, but this Kiwi girl had gotten under his skin.

Daniel opened his eyes, and two blazing blue globes were staring back at him, rich with need.

Soon, Harper, soon you will be mine.

CHAPTER THIRTEEN

"Kiss me," she said, and his lips dropped to hers.

It was a different kiss than the one in the lift, and she knew he was holding back.

Even as his body closed over hers and she arched into his hard cock, she felt resistance.

At some point during the evening, she'd given up not wanting him. Harper had wanted him from the moment she'd seen him in the hotel lobby. Daniel was the most gorgeous man she'd ever seen in her life.

Though he rarely smiled, when he did, it was as if it was only for her. He gave her one hundred percent of his attention and seemed irritated to be interrupted.

No one in her life had ever done that before.

Yes, he was broody and dominant, but it made her feel so safe and protected she wanted to melt into him. When he looked at her, his eyes sparkled with desire, making her feel like the most beautiful woman in existence.

He was like a drug she was unable to resist.

Daniel gripped her face and ended the kiss.

"Harper," he said breathlessly, leaning in and kissing her neck. "I'm not fucking you out here."

"No?" she said, arching into his touch, his mouth hot on her skin.

"I'm just going to stop…" he said, nudging the material of her dress down to expose one of her breasts.

"Oh, God," she cried out softly as his mouth wrapped around her nipple and sucked, nibbled, and licked.

"Jesus, you have gorgeous breasts," Daniel said, pulling the other one out and cupping it. His mouth lowered to that one and sucked harder this time.

"Oh God, Daniel," Harper cried.

His mouth lifted, and he leaned over her again. "Not here, Harper. When we do this, I want you naked, spread wide on the bed so I can taste your pussy and hear you scream."

"Please." She pressed up against him.

"Fucking hell," Daniel said, lowering his forehead to hers.

Then his mouth slammed back over hers, and like teenagers, they clawed at each other through their clothes. When she finally lowered her hand to grasp his cock, his hand gripped her wrist and stopped her.

"Wait," he growled, his breathing labored. Harper stared at him in question. "That's the point of no return, sweetheart. You touch my cock and I'm inside you, fucking you."

"I may not be as experienced as you, but I think that's where this is headed." She smirked.

Daniel bit her lip playfully, and it just made her squirm more.

She watched as he fought his desire and conscience.

"What's wrong?" she asked finally.

"I could easily pull your dress up and fuck you hard right now," Daniel said, his fingers running across the flesh of her ass. "And, Jesus, I am inches from doing it."

"Then do it."

"No. Not out here."

She frowned. "There's no one here, Daniel."

"There could be," he growled. "I'm not having someone see you. See us."

Her head fell back against the pillows.

"So you want to cuddle?" she laughed.

"First time for everything, I guess," Daniel said and lay back down beside her. She turned into him, and their legs entwined.

"What, you've never cuddled?"

"No, Harper, I don't cuddle," he said, brushing hair off her face. "I work. I fuck. I work out. I eat. I work. I fuck…repeat. I don't cuddle."

She frowned. "Everyone needs cuddles."

"Then show me."

Harper nestled into his chest, and Daniel wrapped his arms around her. They wriggled until they both found comfort, despite his erection between them, and she let out a little sigh. "Look at that. You're an expert."

"Go to sleep before I change my mind," he groaned.

Harper smiled and felt herself doze off. The lights and hurricane woke her a handful of times, but when Daniel tightened his arm around her, she'd fall back asleep.

The man she swore she'd run away from.

The man, despite who and what he was, seemed to melt her walls. She knew she'd pay the price for it, eventually, but right now it felt perfect.

Harper woke with a sore head and dry mouth. She realized she'd left the bottles of water inside the hotel suite. The moment she moved Daniel roused beside her.

"I'm just going to get some water," she whispered.

Daniel opened his eyes and stared at her.

Oh God, please tell me he's not going to regret last night. I couldn't handle another rejection.

His eyes blinked and heat filled them. His fingers, where they lay on her body, pressed firmer and she was pulled into him as he took her mouth. "Good morning."

His voice was all gravel, causing a shiver through her body.

"How are you this beautiful, even in the morning?" Daniel asked, his eyes roaming over her.

"Clearly you need glasses."

Daniel sat up, forcing her onto her back, and moaned. "I'm going to get that water for you. Stay there."

"So bossy," she said, then coughed.

Daniel crawled off the mattress and grabbed the swipe card, then disappeared inside her hotel suite.

Harper pulled her phone out of her bag and saw it was eight in the morning. She read the three messages from her mother, who was concerned about the hurricane. She'd replied to a few messages during the evening but ignored one of her calls.

Harper would pay for that.

Ping.

Hey girl. You're online!

What are you doing awake so early on a Saturday?

She replied to Kristen. New Zealand was twenty-three hours ahead, making it seven in the morning.

I was a little worried about you, so didn't sleep very well. I've been checking the news.

Oh babe, thank you, but we are okay.

We?

Crap. **Collective 'we.'**

Who is he? Spill.

Harper grinned. She wasn't ready to tell anyone about Daniel yet. Even her best friend.

He was complicated and if it lasted more than tonight, she'd be lucky to even call it a holiday romance.

There was also the fact they would be in the same business meetings tomorrow and over the next few days, so Harper knew she had to separate the two things in her head.

There was a very strong chemistry between them that neither of them could deny. Well, except Daniel last night. It had surprised her. She thought he'd be the kind of man to just rip her clothes off and take what he wanted no matter who saw.

She did like that he hadn't. Except for the dull ache between her legs that wouldn't go away.

She squeezed her thighs together and rolled onto her tummy, propping the phone on the pillow.

God, she needed him soon, or she'd be self-servicing. Something she'd learned to do after David left.

Maybe a man like Daniel could show her things no previous lover had.

No one. Stop being a detective LOL. I have to jump in the shower and be a Hawaiian Goddess now. Talk to you later.

I will break you down, Harper Kāne. Go shag whoever he is all day long.

Harper burst into laughter as Daniel stepped back into the hallway. He looked at her in question and she grinned, taking the bottle of water from him and slugging it down.

A text to Akino and scroll through the news, and they learned the hurricane had moved away from the island.

Harper leaned over the lanai, the Hawaiian term for balcony, and they'd seen the carnage on the roads and beaches below them. Mostly it was fronds from the palm trees and rubbish, but there were also pieces of signage and a few other obvious bits of damage.

Many of the stores had used sandbags for protection, and the buzz as they cleaned up was easy to hear, even from the 45th floor.

Harper liked to think she was assisting Daniel in moving the mattress back inside the room, but in the end, he'd told her to let go and he'd pulled with force until it landed back on the base in her new bedroom.

It had been worth it to watch his muscles bunch and swell, and the sweat between his pecs.

Now, as Daniel stood and turned to her, she saw him recognize the look in her eyes.

Harper bit her lip

He stepped closer.

"Oh, no," Harper said, stepping away. "I need to brush my teeth."

"Harper, I spent all night kissing you." Daniel frowned.

She turned to run to the bathroom but felt his arms around her. She squealed as his mouth landed on his. Suddenly she didn't care about Colgate or toothbrushes or any damn thing. She melted into his embrace and moaned.

"God, I love hearing you make that sound," he said against her lips and began to push the straps off her dress.

His mouth moved down her neck, pushing the dress down until he found her bare nipple.

"Fuck," she groaned.

Daniel pushed the rest of her dress to the ground, and she stood there in just a pair of black lace panties. His eyes burned as he took in her body.

She began to quiver with nervousness and need.

"Jesus, Harper," he said, wiping his hand over his mouth. Her eyes darted to his, and he cupped her face. "You are so fucking beautiful."

When she went to speak, his thumb landed on her bottom lip and rubbed along it.

"I'm going to fuck you. Are you on board with this?" he asked, and she nodded. Maybe she'd nodded a little too much, but fuck being over eager. She wanted this man inside her, on her, over her, under her.

She placed her hands on his chest and Daniel stayed her hands. "I'm going to need you to not touch anything for a few minutes or I might lose control."

Harper swallowed.

When his lips landed on hers again, she leaned into him, only to be lifted and placed on the bed. Daniel leaned over her, breathing her in.

"I don't ever remember wanting a woman this damn much," he said as his mouth began a slow, torturous path down her body. He sucked both nipples as she arched up and when he got to her hips, his palm was spread over her stomach.

The other took her panties and slid them off.

Harper drew in a long, sharp breath, and their eyes met. White fire danced in his light blue eyes, igniting her body even more.

"Open for me, Harper," Daniel ordered as he spread her thighs.

She felt exposed and vulnerable, and her body trembled. She swallowed, and he leaned down to kiss her again.

"Okay?"

She nodded.

He moved between her legs, his fingers pressing into her wet flesh.

"Oh, God," she cried, her body tensing, needing more.

"Relax for me. I've been wanting to do this for days. I want to hear you scream, Harper. Scream my name. You got that?"

Her body trembled as she obeyed the gorgeous man on top of her.

CHAPTER FOURTEEN

Daniel dropped his mouth to the gorgeous wet pink flesh between him.

She was so sweet he let out a moan of his own.

Sweet Jesus.

She was like a damn drug. The way she looked at him, her laugh, her lips, those eyes.

Her pussy.

He ran his finger around skillfully, circling her clit, and held her down with his other hand. Sucking and licking, he felt her quivering around his mouth. Then he pressed a finger inside and she was like a wild horse bolting.

This woman had been missing out on good fucking all her life. Daniel was looking forward to changing that.

"Let go, baby, feel it all."

"Oh, God," she cried.

Two fingers now and he was working her as his tongue flicked over her clit. He felt her body convulse, and the orgasm ripped from her throat.

She cried out his name as he reached inside his shorts and stroked himself.

Daniel needed to be inside her.

He stood, one hand on her knee. "Stay open for me, baby."

As he pulled off his shorts, his eyes flicked between her flushed face and her swollen pink pussy."

"Fuck, you are gorgeous."

He tore open a condom and positioned himself between her legs.

He was hard, erect and fucking ready to be inside her. Nudging her entrance, he held her bright blue eyes. "Tell me you are okay to keep doing this."

Fuck, if she said no, he would go insane. Harper nodded, and he nearly cursed. She gripped his arms and dug her sharp wee nails into him as he pressed against her entrance.

"You're bigger than—"

He growled. "Don't. No one else is allowed in here with us. This is just you and me, baby."

Baby?

He'd never called anyone baby. It just kept falling out.

As she nodded, he took her lips in his and pressed inside. She gasped against his mouth, but he kept working inside her, kissing her, owning her. Then he was fully wrapped in her hot, sweet pussy.

They gasped and stared, panting, needing, and then he began to move. Harper clenched him as he thrust slowly at first until intense hot pleasure spread throughout his entire body.

Then he sped things up. Pounding her, Harper pressed into him, moving with him, and it struck him she was as sexual as he was. He lifted her up to him, onto his knees, and she grabbed his shoulder.

"Shit, fuck, oh God," she cried as he accessed her g-spot. "Daniel, you…oh fuck."

As she tightened around him, his own release rose to the surface. God, she felt so fucking incredible.

"Harper, I want you to come. Now. On my cock." He growled the order. She tossed her head back and cried out his name.

Daniel's fingers dug into the flesh on her ass and rode them to the moment of pure fucking ecstasy.

Then he collapsed.

Daniel sipped his coffee, watching the guests surface from the unsettled, stormy night. Many had bags under their eyes and looked worse for wear.

Opposite him, Harper glowed as she demolished her eggs benedict. Fuck, she was gorgeous. And sexy. He already wanted her again.

"What?" she said, her fork halfway to her mouth.

"I'm just enjoying watching you eat." He laughed when she frowned. "Women in New York…never mind."

He realized his error as soon as he'd said the words.

"Are you calling me fat, Daniel Dufort?" she teased.

"No. I think you're the most sexy and gorgeous woman I've ever had breakfast with," he said, lifting his coffee to his lips and meaning every damn word.

Harper kept eating, clearly more concerned with her hunger than his attempt to compliment her. He liked her even more for it.

Because he *did* like her. He liked Harper way too fucking much. In fact, this was the first breakfast he'd ever shared with a woman he'd had sex with and found he didn't want her to go.

Anywhere.

Daniel wasn't sure what Harper wanted or where she saw this going, and he felt slightly powerless.

This was unfamiliar territory for him.

And the timing was fucking terrible.

He'd told her he was single, and he was. It had been the truth. There was no need for Harper to know about the shit storm back home. He had no wife, no girlfriend, and no lover.

And had no intention of having one either, but while he was in Hawaii, he wanted more of Harper. He wanted to fuck her. Many more times.

And talk to her.

And listen to her laugh.

And stare at her.

No doubt all this was an irrational reaction to potentially losing his bachelor status.

As far as Daniel was concerned, the two situations were completely separate.

Harper was his while in Hawaii.

The Mackenzie bullshit would be dealt with one way or another.

Daniel swirled his coffee.

Yeah, okay, it probably wasn't that black and white. If it did progress, for some inconceivable reason, Harper would hear about it. It would probably hurt her, as she'd believed he was with Nadia while they had been together. Which was a fair assumption. A man rarely got engaged overnight.

Of course, her assumption would be wrong, but by the time she heard it, she would be back in New Zealand and trying to explain or justify it would be impossible. If he ended up having to marry Nadia, he would be unable to tell anyone the truth.

But right now he had the opportunity to fix this, and fuck yes, he was doing everything he could to ensure he remained an unmarried man and exposed this corrupt Senator.

Even with the risk to Harper, Daniel found he could not walk away. He wanted more of Harper in every single way.

She glanced up at him as she placed her utensils on the plate. "You okay?"

"Yes." Daniel nodded, but something tightened in his chest. He didn't want to hurt her. If he was a decent man, he would throw his napkin onto the plate and wish her a good day. He'd thank her for a wonderful evening—and morning—and say he'd see her at the business meeting tomorrow.

But clearly, he was not a decent man. He was an asshole.

"What are your plans today?" Daniel asked instead.

Total asshole.

Harper stared at him, her mouth slightly open, surprised. He wondered if she might say she was busy.

He cleared his throat, feeling oddly vulnerable.

"I'm going to the Ala Moana Mall," Harper said. "You?"

"Do you like shopping?" he asked.

"Of course, I have a big list."

"Where is this list?" he grinned. Daniel would buy her every fucking thing she wanted. Then drag her home to bed.

"Up here." She tapped the side of her head.

"I don't believe it. You seem more of a planner than that," he said, smirking at her.

"Okay, fine," she said and pulled out her phone, opening her notes app. "Here's my real list, but there are some things in my head, too."

He took the phone and ran his eyes over all the brands, products, and shops Harper wanted to visit. They were all mainstream brands, but he wasn't surprised.

He glanced up at her, knowing there was no way this independent woman would let him buy her anything, but he could do his best.

Daniel contemplated heading up to work but found he had no desire to do that for the first time in…ever.

"We just don't have half these stores in New Zealand, so it's a treat to shop in Hawaii. Not that you'd understand. I bet you have a personal shopper."

"Yes." He nodded

"That's half the fun. I could never have someone buy my clothing." Harper shrugged.

Daniel disagreed but let out a small laugh, then his phone beeped.

"Excuse me a minute," he said, and checked the message. It was nothing urgent—at least nothing that would pull him out of the spell this woman had put him under. Strangely, Daniel was enjoying it.

Cuddling Harper last night had felt warm and delicious. He felt as if he'd been protecting her, and that made him feel powerful.

He was familiar with that feeling, but this felt different. More substantial. The way it did when he'd stood next to his brothers on the playground fighting bullies.

Daniel put his phone down, dabbed his mouth with his napkin, and dropped it onto his plate.

"Well, then. Shall we go?"

"Yes," Harper said, standing. Then she looked up. "Wait. Go where?"

He smiled and put a hand in his pocket.

"You want to come shopping with me?" she asked. "To Ala Moana."

"Anywhere you want to go," Daniel said, placing his hand on her lower back and leading them out of the restaurant.

Harper nearly tripped over herself. She was so flabbergasted. He grinned.

"I'm not sure…"

"Except lingerie shopping. If you start trying on those little things, I will fuck you in the changing rooms," he said, whispering into her hair.

Her mouth dropped open, and she blushed.

Brightly.

The lift door closed as they made their way back up to their rooms.

"Daniel?"

He felt her discomfort and turned. She wasn't saying no to him. He was taking her shopping, and that was that. She must know he was a man who got what he wanted, and he wanted Harper.

"I don't shop at the same places as you. I, well, obviously I'm not a billionaire."

A different kind of blush crept over her face now. It was shame, and it irritated him in a way he'd never felt before.

"Harper," he said quietly and took her hand, pulling her against him. He stared down at her. "I'm fully aware of that. You can rest assured I am not after you for your money."

She let out a little laugh. "Well, that's good because I was beginning to wonder."

He hated seeing her so ashamed.

"Just don't go all *Pretty Woman* on me and I'll be fine." His brows bunched in confusion. "Seriously? Julia Roberts. Rodeo Drive?"

He shook his head.

"Never mind. Just keep your thingy in your pants."

This time, his brows shot to his hairline.

"Wallet, Daniel. Your wallet." Then she grinned. "And the other thing."

The lift doors opened. "No promises on either of those things." He walked her to her penthouse, swiped the card, and opened the door. "I'll be back in twenty minutes."

Daniel kissed her with force, then left her rubbing her lips.

CHAPTER FIFTEEN

To say Harper was nervous about going shopping with a billionaire was an understatement. She couldn't imagine him being impressed with her excitement at buying things from Gap or digging through the shelves at Ross Outlet stores, where you could get a ton of great deals on basic designer brands.

Heck, he'd probably want to go into all the designer shops, which she enjoyed the thrill of, but it was just a bit more uncomfortable when you were with someone who could buy the damn company.

She assumed.

Harper was tempted to Google exactly how rich Daniel was, but decided against it.

She didn't want to think about it. Her body still ached from the delicious orgasms she'd had this morning. She could feel Daniel all over her body and wanted to just sit and smile like an idiot.

He had been such an incredible lover. His mouth, his fingers, his eyes, the way they had held hers and taken in every inch of her.

Daniel didn't smile often, but when he did, it nearly bowled her over. Yet his eyes were so talkative and emotive. They said what he wouldn't.

She sensed he liked her.

She liked him way too much.

She'd ignore her insecurities and go shopping with him because the thought of spending a whole day was much more delicious than missing him.

And she knew she would.

She only had a short amount of time with Daniel in Hawaii and however long they chose to continue doing this was something she was willing to make the most of.

Quickly, she raced to her half-unpacked suitcase and dug through it for something to wear. She pulled out a pair of cut-off shorts, a white cotton halter neck top, and a pair of sneakers.

She ripped off her dress and stood in front of the mirror, updating her makeup and fluffing her hair. Then she pulled out her toothbrush and gave them a second brush for the day.

Because Daniel.

As she stood staring at her body, she remembered the feel of his mouth on her breasts. Her hand went to her hard nipple.

Groan.

She squeezed.

How could she want him again already?

She felt the heat pool between her legs and moisture slip into her panties.

"Oh, God."

She dropped the toothbrush and spat, then walked back into the bedroom and stood staring at her clothes. Her hand slipped into her panties as she stared at the clock.

There was no way she could spend the day with Daniel with so much need burning within her.

She leaned over, her hand on the headboard as her other hand rubbed on her clit.

"Fuck," she cried.

Knock, knock.

Oh God, no.

Harper glanced at the clock on the side table and saw the time.

"Shit, shit, shit."

Harper raced into the bathroom and grabbed a towel, wrapping it around herself. Despite the bra and panties underneath.

She ran to the door and took a few breaths, then pulled it open.

"Hey, sorry. Nearly ready."

Daniel stood there in all his glory. Tall, big, powerful. A pair of sunglasses sat on his head, and he'd had a shave. In a short-sleeved pale blue shirt that fit his large chest perfectly and a pair of beige shorts, Harper nearly jumped him.

Their eyes met, and she knew he knew.

He stepped into her space, letting the door close behind them. His fingers tugged the towel, and it dropped to the floor.

"What held you up?" he asked low.

"The, um, the…"

"Are you wet right now?" he asked in a low growl. "Don't lie to me."

Fire blazed through her body to her core, and she swallowed and nodded.

Daniel lifted her onto a nearby table and she let out a ridiculous sound. Then her panties were ripped off.

"Good girl for telling me," he said as he dropped to the floor and pushed her legs wide.

"Oh, God," she said in a loud sigh as his mouth engulfed her entire pussy. His fingers followed, and his eyes lifted to hers as he pleasured her with every touch, lick, and suction of his mouth.

She felt like a complete sex maniac needing this man like a drug. It was as if her body had just woken up and couldn't get enough of him.

"Eyes on mine," he growled as his tongue swirled in circles on her clit.

"Fuck, Daniel," she panted.

He finger fucked her while he held her eyes. "While we are together, I don't want you touching yourself. Do you understand?"

She nodded.

But what the fuck?

"I will pleasure you, and only me. Your orgasms are mine," he said, then sped up his tongue action on her clit.

She burst apart.

He ripped off his shorts, snapped on a condom, and pulled her off the table, spinning her.

"Hands out," he said, nudging her over the table. "That's it."

She felt his cock at her entrance, then he plunged into her.

"I fuck you. No one else," he said, pounding possessively. "Not even you."

Harper cried out as he continued his dominating demands. When he was spent, he pulled out and lifted her with care. His mouth was on hers as he carried her into the bedroom and lay with her on the bed.

"Are you okay?" he asked.

She nodded.

"I meant what I said," Daniel said, running his fingers over her still hard nipple. "You make me insane, Harper. I need to have all of you."

Daniel opened the car door and Harper slid into the *Tesla Model X.*

Without saying anything, he pulled out of the hotel parking lot, and they drove through Waikiki to the large shopping mall. He had been quieter than normal since they'd had sex the second time.

So had she.

Harper wondered what it meant.

They hit a set of lights just before the mall and he turned, taking her hand. "Are you comfortable with this?" Daniel asked.

"Shopping with you?"

"No," Daniel answered, and she knew what he meant.

She glanced away. "I mean, it's intense."

"I am a dominant man." He replied. "But you do something to me, Harper. This is new to me, too."

"Yes, but this is my body," she responded and watched Daniel's hand grip the steering wheel firmly. The lights turned green, and his free hand slid up the middle of her legs.

"Your orgasms are mine," he said. "If I want to make you wet and wait, if I want to make you come right now, then I need you to let me do that."

Her panties were instantly wet again, and she squirmed in the leather seat.

"Daniel, stop," she said, placing her hand on his. "I can't…"

"You will."

He removed his hand and soon they were parked in an underground parking lot. Daniel turned to her. "Tell me what you need."

An orgasm, but Harper wasn't going to say that. He didn't own her body. She did. If she needed relief, she would damn well give it to herself. He might be in charge of everyone in his world, but Daniel didn't own her.

"Nothing."

He arched a brow and her eyes dropped to his visibly hard cock. She wasn't the only one in need here.

Harper looked back at him and pressed her lips together in a smile, but the stubborn, gorgeous man simply stared back at her with his icy blue eyes knowingly.

"Say the word and I'll drive us home. Then it's yours. But Harper, without your words, you will have to wait."

Nope, she wasn't going to give in.

Powerful men like him needed boundaries, even if she was going to spend the day squirming.

She lifted her eyes to his. "Let's go shopping."

Despite need pulsing within her, which made concentrating very difficult, Harper successfully purchased a handful of things over the past two hours.

She'd taken a moment to slip her hand between her legs while trying on a dress in Kate Spade, but Daniel had been standing outside the dressing room, and as if he'd known, had called out, "Harper."

She'd let out a silent scream, then opened the door. He'd stepped in and taken her mouth.

"Buy it," he'd demanded without even looking.

CHAPTER SIXTEEN

Daniel leaned his arm on the counter as Harper swiped her card yet again. It was taking a lot of willpower not to hand over his black Amex with every purchase.

Neither of them were really focused on shopping, and they both knew it. It was a battle of wills and if Harper thought he wasn't aware of it, she was kidding herself.

Daniel played these games every fucking day. He did give her ten points for effort, though. He could tell she was dying for his cock inside her, and he wasn't being an asshole for saying so.

He wanted her just as damn much.

Daniel loved how sexually charged Harper was, and how his every touch was driving her insane.

They stepped onto the escalator, and he ran his hand down her back, letting it sit on her ass as he tugged her closer. When she glanced up at him, he lowered his lips to touch hers gently.

Her jolty breaths went straight to his dick.

"Shall we go home?" he grinned.

"No," she said stubbornly, and he cursed under his breath, then grinned. He loved her resilience, but Daniel didn't know how much of his own he had left in him.

Why hadn't he met a woman who made him feel like this before?

He'd said his need to possess her came from being such a dominant man, which was true, but never had he felt this obsessed.

Or obsessed at all.

It was very new.

He brushed his hand over her hair and Harper leaned into him.

God, she felt amazing.

Sex aside, Harper fit. Like trying on a custom-made suit or a half-million-dollar watch and thinking, *fuck yes,* this is perfect. She fit against him, around his cock, and in his arms.

Daniel glanced down at her shopping bags, some of which he carried, and made a decision. Harper wasn't going home without a piece of him to remember.

He might not be able to keep her forever, but she meant something to him.

He just wasn't sure why.

Or how she'd got inside her heart

They grabbed some ice-cold drinks, both of them feeling the heat of the day and the miles they'd walked. Harper dropped to the steps outside Neiman Marcus, so he sat beside her.

"Are you actually enjoying yourself? I can't tell."

"Watching you, yes," he answered honestly and lifted the bottle to his lips.

"Do you want to buy anything while we're here?"

Daniel stared out at the stores in front of them. "Yes. But I'm going to need your help."

"Shoot."

"A birthday gift. For a family member. A woman," he said. "Around our age."

Harper narrowed her eyes. "Like older or younger."

"Twenty-eight, I think," he said, making it up as he went. "A cousin, twice removed, so she's not—"

"A billionaire?" Harper asked, laughing.

"Right." Christ, this felt way too easy.

"Is she a corporate woman?"

He shrugged.

"A mom?"

"No," Daniel said. "A teacher, I think."

God, it was like he was a professional liar.

"Something practical would be good," Harper said, standing.

Damn. That wasn't at all where he was trying to lead this. He scrambled for something else.

"So, her husband died." *Christ, he was burying himself.* "I thought I'd get her something special."

"Like jewelry?" He nodded, and she shook her head. "That seems romantic."

Romantic? Is that what he was doing here?

Nope. Noooo, nope, nope. He just wanted to treat her.

"There can be nonromantic jewelry. Girls love that shit," Daniel said, leading her to the store he wanted to shop at before he could dig himself a deeper hole. "Come on."

They stepped inside *Cartier* and the manager walked up and greeted him personally, shaking his hand. The Dufort family was well known around the world as a hotel dynasty, especially by luxury brands such as this.

"Aloha, Mr. Dufort," the man said and shook his hand.

Harper gave him a look and he winked back at her.

"Aloha."

"Will you just be browsing today, or is there something I can show you?"

"I'm looking for a gift," Daniel replied, purposely glancing at Harper, and the man nodded. This wasn't his first rodeo.

"For his cousin," Harper said, leaning into the conversation. "She's a teacher, so nothing too flashy."

Daniel held back a smile. The manager maintained his professional expression and nodded.

"Let me see what we have that could be suitable. Please look around and I will put together a selection." The man left the two of them alone.

"Wow, you don't even have to find it yourself."

Daniel snorted. He found himself enjoying shopping with Harper.

She grinned at him. "Seriously, though. Our lives are so different."

"Yes." His smile fell. "They are."

Her words felt uncomfortable. All his life he'd known his wealth separated him from others and he'd never cared before this moment. Harper saw him as someone she could never be with outside of this *thing* they had together, and perhaps she was right. But it didn't mean he liked it.

What if he *did* want her?

Theoretically, of course.

A store assistant offered them a glass of champagne, which he declined, and Harper accepted. "When in Rome." She grinned, lifting her flute, then moaned. "Oh God, this is good."

It was probably *Cristal*. They would be expecting him to spend a great deal today and popped the good stuff.

"Moan like that and I'm dragging you home right fucking now, Harper," he said, and her eyes flashed to his.

The manager returned with two trays, interrupting the moment.

"Here we go," he said and laid them out on the cabinets. Harper leaned in and he could see her eyes light up like a kid at Christmas.

Daniel smiled.

This is what he wanted for her.

The first tray contained a range of jewelry in silver. He glanced at Harper's own silver jewelry. This man knew what he was doing.

She picked up a bracelet surrounded with shimmering diamonds, then put it down, swapping it for a ring with three bands all connected—also containing a ring of diamonds. The next bracelet was a wraparound style, with some type of nob on the end.

She quickly dropped that. Clearly not a favorite.

"These are gorgeous," Harper said, looking up at him. "They might be a bit too much for a teacher."

"Everyone likes nice stuff for special occasions," he said.

Harper shrugged. "Not from your cousin."

Was she jealous?

He moved closer and wrapped his arm around her lower back, resting it on her hip. She glanced up at him and he watched the tension fade.

Interesting.

She turned to the next tray where a silver watch sat. The square face was surrounded by diamonds and had black hands.

"You don't wear a watch," he observed, taking it from her.

"No," she said, shrugging. "I used to."

"This is an excellent choice, sir," the manager said and gave him all the statistics on the piece. "It is from our *Panthere De Cartier* collection."

Daniel knew the price wouldn't be mentioned, so he let him rattle on about the workmanship and so on.

"Perhaps you could try it on for Mr. Dufort, so he can see. For his *cousin,*" the manager recommended.

Harper nodded, taking it back.

"Sure." She slipped it onto her fine wrist and Daniel knew immediately he was buying it for her.

It looked stunning.

"Well, it's practical," Harper said, turning her wrist. "Very comfortable."

He smiled.

"She'll need to get it insured with all those diamonds," Harper said, glancing at him. "Or, you know, perhaps you could if she can't afford it."

Shit.

He hadn't thought about that.

It was just another example of how different their worlds were.

"I will take care of it," Daniel said. "It looks lovely on you."

"I think she'll love it." Harper didn't take her eyes off it as she spoke.

The manager cleared his throat.

"I will give you both a moment to make your decision," he said, and left them alone. Daniel was going to make sure this man got a juicy bonus for his performance today.

"Do *you* love it?" he asked, leaning down into her hair. He could tell already, but wanted to be sure.

"Yes, it's exquisite. A timeless piece," Harper said, twisting it back and forth, and he knew she was catching the diamonds in the light so it would sparkle. He might not know her well, but Daniel sensed she was going to be mad when she found out about his deceit.

But she'd forgive him.

It was just a little white lie.

"Good. Then let's get it wrapped up and head back to the hotel," he said and magically the manager appeared and took his black credit card.

He handed her the bag to carry and swing like she had with all her other goodies, but Harper crushed it to her chest.

"Did he even say how much it was?" she asked, and he glanced down at her.

"No. It's a gift. It doesn't matter."

"Make sure you get her the insurance. On a teacher's salary, it might not be affordable," she said, looping her arm through his as they walked to the car.

She was entirely too damn good for him.

And yet, when he got them home, he knew he was ripping her shorts off her and fucking her hard.

CHAPTER SEVENTEEN

Harper opened her eyes and took in the powerful tanned back beside her. They'd been lying on the *Altitude* sun loungers all afternoon, drinking cocktails, and nibbling on taster plates for dinner.

After, that is, Daniel had relieved the hot and torturous ache between her legs.

Harper's bags had barely hit the carpet when Daniel had swept her off her feet and carried her into the bedroom. She'd watched him remove his clothes and hurried to do the same. Daniel had pulled her naked body against his and kissed her like a starving man.

There had been no foreplay. He'd fallen over her and yanked her legs around him. His fingers had circled her juices around her pussy, and then he was inside her.

They'd groaned and cried out, then suddenly frozen while he was deep inside her.

"Shit."

"Shit."

No condom.

"I'm on the pill," she said.

"I'm clean," he added, and shook his head. "Fuck, I'm sorry, Harper. I just damn well wanted you so much."

"Fine, just move, would you?" she'd replied, pulling on his arms.

"Christ." He'd groaned, and soon they were both gasping with the relief they needed.

Now the sun was setting, and the sky was a blend of pinks and blues. Harper basked in the romantic mood that surrounded them, as couples lazily embraced and kissed.

Being a romance author, she took mental notes of all the little details, knowing she'd write about them one day.

Daniel reached over and lifted her hand, kissing her knuckles. She'd blinked at him, surprised by the affectionate gesture.

"Aren't you worried someone will see us?" she asked, looking around at all the staff and guests. He was a well-known billionaire, after all.

"No," he replied, but he blinked, and she got the feeling he was hiding something.

The next morning, she woke in Daniel's bed. There'd been no discussion about whether they would spend the night together. He'd simply held her tight until they'd fallen asleep.

Harper had smiled at how good he was getting at cuddling.

Today they were meeting with *BookFlix* at 10:00 a.m. and she needed to get ready. She kissed his back, and he stirred.

"I'm going to shower," she said, slipping out of bed. "I'll see you at the meeting."

"Stop. I need to taste you before you leave," he growled and immediately she felt herself get wet.

"There's no time," she said, scrambling away.

"Harper," he warned, but she blew him a kiss and backed out of the bedroom.

"See you downstairs at ten."

The last thing she saw was Daniel wiping his hand over his hair, looking frustrated.

As she ran along the hallway to her penthouse suite, Harper wondered if all holiday romances were this intense.

An hour later, Harper stood in the living room wearing a work dress. She placed her laptop on the armchair along with her purse and slid lip gloss over her lips.

Tap, tap.

She opened the door and found Daniel standing in front of her wearing a white shirt and a long pair of black pants. Holy shit, he looked gorgeous and every bit the powerful CEO.

"I thought…" she said, but he stepped inside and shut the door.

"You look sexy as hell," Daniel said, his eyes running over her body.

She swallowed.

"I thought I was meeting you downstairs?" Harper asked, but she could see the fire in his eyes. "Daniel?"

He took a few more steps toward her as she retreated. "No. You said we were meeting downstairs. I have other plans."

"For?" But she knew.

He continued stalking her until her legs banged against the back of the sofa. "I want to know your pussy is screaming out for me while I can't touch you this morning. I want to know you'll be wet and that I'm still able to pleasure you."

She swallowed.

What was he talking about? They would be in a meeting.

"Daniel," she said, placing a hand on his chest. "I need to focus during this meeting."

"You will," he said. "But you'll also feel pleasure. My pleasure."

Harper wasn't sure what he meant, but if he planned to tease her, then leave, she would just shake it off and focus.

Daniel reached down and slid his hand under her skirt. "Take your panties off and go sit at the coffee table," he instructed. "I have something for you."

Oh, God.

She hesitated.

"Harper," he growled, running his hand up and down his hard cock through his pants. He took her chin in his hand and said firmly, but thick with desire, "Now."

God damn him. She was now sopping wet and her nipples hard as hell, so she figured if he could quickly make her come, then it would be worth it.

They'd just have to be a few minutes late.

She lifted her dress and sat on the table, pulling her panties off.

"Leave the shoes. Feet up either side of me," he ordered, sitting down in front of her.

"Daniel, if you don't make me come, I swear to God," she said even as she did as she was told. She felt less vulnerable about her pussy being exposed to him now.

"Good girl," he said, touching her wetness as his eyes held hers. "Now," Daniel said, pulling something out of his pocket. "These are for you."

In his hand were two round balls connected to a string.

Her eyes widened.

What was he planning to do with those?

"Lie back." His hand went to her stomach, and he nudged her back. "I'm going to put these inside you, and if I think you deserve pleasure today, I will turn them on."

"Dan...ohmyGoddd." She said as he rubbed the solid objects around the entrance of her pussy.

"Relax as they go in," he said and pressed. With a pop they went in, and Harper tensed and let out a cry.

"Oh God, Daniel, you can't—"

"Yes, I can. And I have," Daniel said, leaning over her and lapping at her open mouth. "How does that feel?"

She wanted to lie, but she couldn't. "Damn you, it's good, so good."

His heated eyes held hers as his fingers circled her clit and she arched into his touch, her body trembling.

"Don't come. Not yet."

Damn him.

Then he stood and held out a hand. Harper took it, confused, as he pulled her to her feet and suddenly a vibration began within her. Her legs buckled as she cried out, but Daniel caught her.

Oh, my God.

"Daniel, Jesus, I can't focus with these inside me."

He palmed her breast and took her mouth in his, kissing her deeply. She melted into him as the vibration whirled within her.

"Will you do as you're told and leave them in?" he asked, taking her chin in his fingers with one hand and pressing his other through her wet pussy.

She swallowed and nodded.

The vibration turned off. Daniel bent down and pulled her panties back up. Then the two of them stood staring at each other.

One part of her wanted to tell him he was mad, the other loved this naughty game. Even as she felt out of her mind with the need for release.

"Good girl."

Harper bit her bottom lip and Daniel glanced at it, drew a breath, then walked to the door.

"During the meeting—" Daniel began.

"You don't need to say it," Harper interrupted him. He was going to tell her to be professional and not let anyone know they were sleeping together.

Part of her was irritated he even thought he had to say it.

"Not for me. For you, Harper."

She frowned.

"Rubbish. The last thing you want is a media company knowing who you're fucking."

Daniel shrugged. "Maybe, but I also want them to respect you, as this is an important moment in your career."

"Then you might want to play nicely with your damn toy," she said, raising a brow.

"You can handle it." he winked and walked out the door.

Harper shook her head. She felt like she was in a daze but quickly tidied herself up, and by ten she was downstairs where Akino greeted her and led her toward the conference room.

She had met the *BookFlix* team via video conference many times in the past few months, so they weren't strangers, but her tummy still had a few butterflies.

The fact she had a sex toy inside her vagina wasn't helping to calm her nerves, or the fact she'd be sitting in a meeting with Daniel, pretending he was a business associate.

Not someone with the ability to turn on the damn sexy toy.

Everything should go fine.

Just fiiiine.

How was this her life?

Harper had received a video call from Kristen after she had finished her shower earlier.

"Hey, Kris!" Harper had said. "Let me prop you up on my counter so I can talk to you while I do my makeup."

"Hey, girl," Kristen said. "Wow, look at your tan. Are you excited about today?"

Harper took a critical look at herself. Being half Hawaiian, she knew she was blessed to have her golden skin, but Kristen was right. She was looking really tanned now.

"Yes. Excited, and nervous," she replied. "I just hope I can convince them to leave in some of the hotel scenes. They are really key to the character development."

Kristen nodded and lifted a glass of red liquid, which Harper recognized as her daily power smoothie.

"You've got this, babe. You're no pushover. But they are the tv experts, so maybe meet them in the middle," she said. "Don't let it stress you out so much you don't enjoy this amazing opportunity."

Kris was right. She could be such a stress bunny over fine details that she didn't stop to smell the roses.

Right now she had a big, six-foot-three distraction and Harper realized she hadn't been worrying as much.

"True," she murmured.

"So, was the hurricane scary?"

Harper nodded. "Yes, a little. We had to sleep out in the corridor."

Kristen gasped. "Ugh, with strangers?"

Well, yes.

She nodded and laughed.

"Oh my God, did you hate it?" Kristen asked. "Did you sleep?"

She blushed. "It was fine."

"Harper Kāne. What aren't you telling me?" she asked, narrowing her eyes.

Damn best friends—they saw through everything.

"Just taking your advice." She giggled.

"Nooooo. Whooo? Tell me everything!" Kristen squealed.

Harper grinned so wide, she even laughed at herself in the mirror while trying to apply mascara. "Stop or I'll look like a clown by the time I'm finished."

"Spill, girl."

Harper pulled out her hair and began brushing it. "Don't tell a soul."

"Who am I going to tell? Frank from fucking accounting?"

Harper burst out laughing.

"Not even Frank," she said, wondering who Frank was, except obviously the guy in accounting. "I met Daniel Dufort, and we have been...I guess sleeping together."

"You guess? Either you have or haven't," Kristen asked. "Wait, who is Daniel Dufort?"

Oh. Right.

Not everyone on the planet knew who he was.

"Dufort Hotels. The billionaire." Even as the words came out, Harper hated the taste of them on her lips. She had no problem with the fact he was wealthy but describing him by his bank balance just felt wrong.

"The family from New York?" Kristen asked, as she was clearly googling. "Hot damn, girl, he is, my God. I am so proud of you."

Harper shook her head, smiling. "That's a dumb thing to say."

"Why? He's rich, hot and successful." Kristen shrugged. "You could have chosen a bartender instead."

"Speaking of. How's Jeremy?" she asked about the guy Kris had been casually seeing for about six months.

"Don't even ask. All he does is work, go to the gym, and occasionally drop by for sex. It's not a relationship. I know that."

Harper stopped and looked at her friend on the screen. "That's good, babe. You deserve better."

"We both do," Kristen said.

"How about we come back to Hawaii together in a few months? I'll have my payment by then and we can do touristy things and flirt with cute American boys."

"Men, darling. Men." Kristen winked.

She laughed and dabbed on her lip gloss. "Time's up, BFF. I have to fly. Wish me luck."

"Luck!"

When Harper hung up, she'd stood for a moment thinking about their conversation. To Kris, Daniel was a faceless man she was having a fling with.

She didn't feel like that about him. When he was deep inside her, it felt like he owned every part of her. Sure, she wasn't very experienced in casual sex, but the way Daniel looked at her, it didn't feel like *nothing*. He'd admitted he was dominant and possessive, and he was. Perhaps she was reading into it far too much.

This was the kind of silly thinking that would get her hurt.

Now she stood on the other side of the door, about to step into a meeting with this powerful man. And her business partner, *BookFlix*.

Both important.

But only one would remain in her life at the end of her holiday.

That she needed to remember.

"Ms. Kāne," Akino said when he opened the door, announcing her arrival.

"Harper," Denise said, stepping forward and shaking her hand before she could see farther into the room. "It's so lovely to meet you in person."

"Hello, Denise. Thank you again. This is such a privilege," Harper said, thanking the network executive for the millionth time.

Denise waved her away. "You know Thomas, Marissa, and Kas," she said, indicating her team.

"Yes, hello," Harper said, stepping closer to the table and shaking all their hands. They were all familiar faces from the video conferences and emails.

But it was the face down at the end of the room whose eyes were burning into her skin that held her attention.

"Have you met Mr. Dufort?" Denise asked.

Harper blushed. "Yes."

"Ms. Kāne and I are acquainted, thank you, Denise," Daniel said and stood, taking her hand in his, rubbing his thumb discretely over her wrist. "Harper, this is Harry from our marketing team. He will be your primary contact on this project after today."

Of course, because he was returning to New York and his entire life, which didn't include her.

"Hi," she said to Harry.

"Nice to meet you, Harper," Harry said, reaching out his hand. "I love your books, by the way. I am a big fan."

Harper grinned. She never tired of hearing that.

"Thank you so much."

As everyone echoed their love of her books, her eyes darted to Daniel. He looked proud, which surprised her. They had talked little about her writing or books, which was unusual, as most people had a thousand questions when they met an author.

She opened her laptop and glanced up. Dark intense eyes were watching her. Harper cleared her throat, and the corner of his lips curled up.

"Kas, would you like to kick us off?" Denise said, reclining in her chair.

"Yes," the petite blonde said, casting a blushing smile Daniel's way. When he didn't react, the woman cleared her throat and continued.

Harper watched the interaction, realizing this was Daniel's life every day. Women offering themselves to him in subtle—or less subtle—ways because of his position, money, and power.

It wasn't like she hadn't known but watching it in action was another thing. Especially when Daniel had had his fingers inside her just minutes before.

Harper's eyes fell onto her keyboard as Kas started outlining their day.

She wondered if this was why Daniel was interested in her? Harper had done the exact opposite. Was she just a challenge? They say men liked the hunt. Is that what this was?

She looked back at the *BookFlix* woman. Kas was gorgeous and around her age. A rising star in an influential role in entertainment. An American. She had a rock star figure and cascading sexy blonde hair that all the men loved.

"How does that sound, Harper?" Kas asked.

No idea. She hadn't heard a thing.

Harper smiled and looked at the screen on the wall with the agenda projected on it. She sped read through it and nodded.

"Great. Really great," she said, avoiding Daniel's eyes. She could feel him looking at her and the thickness of the sex balls filling her.

Everything was just so confusing and conflicting in her brain right now.

"Shall we jump straight into the filming location then, so Mr. Dufort can get back to his day?" Kas said, giving him a smile worthy of a Colgate advertisement.

Daniel nodded.

"My morning is clear, and Harper has my full commitment to this project, so no need to rush on my behalf," he said, then met her eyes. They had an intensity to them that said *whatever you are thinking—stop it.*

She gave him a little smile and as she began to type on her notepad, a low vibration began.

Shit.

Her body lit up and she squirmed in the chair. She bit the side of her mouth and attempted to tap something on her notepad. It read *Dfsp dpriek spriek psida.* So that would be useful to refer back to.

"Marissa," Denise said, and Harper jumped unnecessarily.

Everyone looked at her, then carried on.

Daniel smiled at her with his eyes.

Fuck.

"So we're looking at book one, obviously. *High Stakes.* It will be seven episodes," Marissa said, pulling up a slide. "We've secured the three beach spots for filming in April through mid-May, and several of the bars and restaurants."

Harper glanced at Daniel again and found his eyes boring into her. His jaw was tight as he shifted in his chair. This was clearly as difficult for him as it was for her.

The need to cry out, as the vibration massaged the inside of her pussy, was close. Harper's mouth parted, and he looked away.

Oh, God.

"The *Hawaii Film Studio* is already booked for some of the scenes we need," Thomas said. "But we are just locking in the final two or three. We may need to rethink those."

The vibration finally turned off.

Harper coughed. "It's, um, essential we don't drop the plane scene. It's really key. It just won't work anywhere else, nor make sense."

It was one of her pain points and she was grateful to Daniel for turning off the toy at the moment he had.

Denise leaned forward. "We understand, Harper, but they don't have a film set for it here, and if we have to find something in LA or hire a private jet, it's going to blow the budget. Let's keep talking about it and see what happens."

Which was code for *it's not going to happen, and we'll break it to you at the last minute.*

Harper ground her teeth and nodded. She didn't want to be the dramatic author who caused problems, but she owed it to her readers to ensure the integrity of the story—its essence—was kept as true as possible.

"I look forward to hearing what the solution will be."

"As for the hotel, Harry and I will work for the next few days to find the best rooms with the best light and book them in," Marissa said.

"Let's discuss the PR side of things, Mr. Dufort," Denise said. "What are your concerns? Or any operational ones."

Daniel turned to Harry, who leaned forward an inch. Harper liked how he let the junior executive take the lead.

"Operationally, we see none. It's great to have your team here to lock in the dates early, so during production we will have the least interruption to our guests," Harry said. "The scenes in the lobby will need to be done between midday and three in the afternoon, which is our quietest time."

Everyone nodded and took notes.

Harper glanced at Daniel and found him watching her. His eyes glistened with an emotion she couldn't place.

Then he blinked, and it was gone.

"Mr. Dufort, did you want to cover the PR?" Harry said.

"I have no concerns. Dufort Hotels marketing will promote this in partnership with BookFlix as per our contract, but I'd also like to offer Dufort Waikiki as a venue for the media launch."

Harper's eyes widened.

"Are you aware it will be Thanksgiving weekend?" Denise asked, looking as surprised as Harper.

"Yes," he said. "Waikiki will be buzzing and I'm sure the cast and media won't mind a few days in Hawaii for the event."

Harper hid a smile.

Daniel was smart. By offering Dufort Waikiki as the media venue, he was keeping the media focused on his hotels.

"I think we can work with that," Denise replied. "Harper, looks like you'll be returning to Hawaii before the end of the year."

Oh.

Seeing Daniel beyond this time together had not really occurred to her. It was a stark reminder she needed to keep her emotions in check, and that this was only a holiday romance.

A really damn hot one.

She glanced over at Kat, who was still eyeballing Daniel, and pressed her lips together. Soon Daniel would be back in New York sleeping with his cocktail of rich Manhattan women.

Which was fine. Totally fine.

CHAPTER EIGHTEEN

Daniel stared out across the beach from the lanai of his penthouse. His laptop was open in front of him, but he couldn't focus on shit.

Instead, he was running a movie of his time so far with Harper in his head. She was currently with *BookFlix*, driving to different spots on the island and reviewing them for the upcoming filming of her book.

He had tried to think of a reason to go with her and came up blank. He hated that he'd even thought about it. Since when had he become a needy lover?

Sex. That's what this was. Harper was an incredible lover. He just needed to sink his cock inside her a few more times.

He hardened at the thought of the sex balls inside her and wondered if she had touched herself.

Daniel picked up his phone.

If you were closer, I would turn the toy on. Make sure you behave.

There was something else bothering him.

The way a shadow had crossed her face when the young *BookFlix* women had tried to flirt with him.

He was used to that shit. It meant nothing to him. Did he hate it? No. He disrespected it.

What did these fucking women think he was going to do? Jump across the table and ask them to spread it while he threw money at them and licked their pussy?

Crass? Yes. But fucking come on.

The more he thought about it, the more he remembered how angry he'd felt in the moment watching Harper, who was clearly upset. He'd wanted to drag her out of the room and tell her…what?

What did he want her to know?

That she was important to him?

That he was committed to her for the two weeks they remained on the island? That he'd never touch another female? Until he returned to New York.

Because he would.

Right?

Well, not Nadia Mackenzie. He wasn't sinking his cock into a woman he didn't want, as if he was some God damn man whore. The thought of her in his bed, where Harper had lay while he plowed into her unsheathed, made him nauseous.

Being with Harper skin to skin had been the opposite. He'd never done that with a woman before and fuck, it had taken things to another level.

And not just physically.

Somehow, it had made him feel closer to her on a level that was new. Spilling into her, knowing the risk of creating a life, was terrifying and thrilling.

And completely fucking crazy.

"Shit," Daniel said, slamming the laptop closed.

What if he got her pregnant? Visions of Harper swollen with his child filled overwhelmed him. She'd look fucking gorgeous.

Daniel stood and walked to the edge of the lanai, running his hand over his hair.

Jesus.

He had fucking feelings for this woman. Strong feelings. It was time to admit it was more than just lust.

And wasn't that a fucking mess?

Of all the times this could happen, a woman comes into his world just as his family is being extorted and his marital status is being used as a bargaining chip.

Just fucking brilliant.

Daniel shook his head.

Harper barely trusted men, and he was not her type at all. A holiday romance where commitment wasn't a requirement? Sure. But as a life partner? No.

But was that what he wanted?

Was he looking to commit to Harper? Or would these feeling disappear in a few days? Daniel had no idea. He had never wanted anyone the next day, let alone feel like this.

Actually, I am on my way up in the lift now. Harper text in reply.

Daniel shook off his thoughts and smiled. He was going to have her in his arms in just a few minutes.

He wanted her. He needed her.

Right now.

He headed down the hall just as the lift pinged, and Harper stepped out. She gave him a shy smile as he stepped up and kissed her.

"How did it go?" he asked.

"Good." She nodded and moved away to open the door.

Daniel immediately sensed the distance she was attempting to put between them and frowned.

"Oh, my God! What did you do?" Harper gasped as she stepped inside. Daniel shrugged and placed his hands in his pockets. Around them, every color rose you could imagine, and as many as could fit in vases filled her room.

"Are you crazy?" she said, dropping her bags and laptop, and turning to him.

Yes.

He reached out and pulled her up against his chest. "Right now, yes."

"They're beautiful, thank you," she said, and he dropped his mouth on hers.

"I need you, Harper. Right now." he said. "Are the balls still inside you?"

Her eyes dropped.

"Harper." Had she taken them out? He'd be disappointed if she had, but the truth was, he had no rule over her body. "Did you come?"

She shook her head. "No."

Daniel took her hand and led her into the bedroom, where he removed her dress. He turned on the device and pleasure flared in a flush over her body.

"Oh God, Daniel."

"Let me take care of you," he said and nudged her legs apart, finding her soaked. "You have been a good girl."

He dropped to his knees and licked her clit, holding her legs so she didn't collapse on him. He continued tasting her as the device vibrated within her, and juices began flowing.

"Oh, your pussy likes this, Harper." He reached up and tweaked her nipple.

"OhGodohGodohGod," she began, but he wasn't letting her finish yet.

He stopped and pulled her down on the floor with him. Then stood, leading his cock toward her mouth. "Suck me off and then I will give you a release."

"You're torturing me." Harper cried but followed his instructions.

Her mouth on his cock was like fire. Sucking hard and fast. Eager and needy.

Fuck. He was going to come like a teenager.

Daniel gripped her hair and pumped into her mouth, pulling out and coming over her breasts.

Harper moaned. "Daniel, please."

He lifted Harper to her feet and laid her on the bed, spreading her legs. "I was wrong. I think you're a very bad girl, and now I want you to come."

She was crying for him, moaning. Writhing.

He licked her pussy, drinking in her sweetness, and tugged on the cord. One, then two of the vibrating balls popped out. Daniel tossed them on the bed, and he glanced at his needy Goddess.

"Now, baby, now you come." His mouth covered her pussy, and he sucked and nibbled at her clit.

Harper cried out his name, her body trembling with desire underneath his hands. Daniel wanted to scream with pride at the pleasure he had given her.

And he never wanted anyone else to touch her.

She felt like she belonged with him.

Water flowed over their naked bodies from the three shower heads. "Talk to me." Daniel said.

"About?" Harper said

He glanced down at her. "I saw what you were thinking today."

"What was I thinking, Daniel?" she said, a healthy dose of her sass returning now that he'd pleasured her. "Oh, mighty mind reader."

"Kas. The girl from *BookFlix*,"

Harper's jaw tensed.

"Oh, right," she said, grimacing. "I guess I saw a glimpse into what your life is like normally, huh? Here, in New York, everywhere I imagine."

He wasn't going to lie. "Yes."

"How many women have you slept with?" she asked.

His eyes flew wide open.

"Christ, Harper, don't ask me that," he said, cringing. "I wouldn't ask you that."

Although suddenly he wanted to know. He suspected it was one—maybe two.

Harper's eyes found his. "Five."

Oh.

Who the fuck were the five men? Were they all men?

Daniel shook his head.

"God, I'm sorry I shouldn't even care. This is…"

"This is what?" Daniel demanded, forcing her to finish what she was going to say.

They both knew what this was. Or wasn't. He was being a total asshole, forcing her to say it. Especially when he couldn't.

"Nothing."

"Fuck that, Harper, this is not nothing, and you know it." Daniel growled and cupped her chin.

Her eyes snapped to his. "Then you tell me!"

"I don't fucking know, but it's freaking me out."

Harper stared at him for a long moment and then lay her head on his chest.

They stayed there for a long time, both letting the reality of their situation sink in, but neither of them willing to voice it further.

Not yet.

Not wanting to destroy what they had, knowing life, and their demons, weren't going to let this be possible.

CHAPTER NINETEEN

The next evening, after Harper had finished with *BookFlix,* and he had finished work, Daniel knocked on her door.

"Ready?"

"Yes. Are you going to tell me where we are going?"

He was taking her out on a date. A proper date. This may only be temporary between them, but Daniel had never felt like this about a woman, and he may never again.

He still hadn't heard anything from Josh Hawke. This afternoon, he'd spent an hour on a video call with Fletcher and Olivia discussing PR angles and was feeling slightly agitated.

Correction; very fucking agitated.

Daniel hated to admit it, even to himself, but his confidence in coming out the other side of this a single man was dropping.

He was also starting to feel pangs of guilt about Harper, even though, technically, it had nothing to do with her. And he wasn't doing anything wrong. But if she heard he got engaged when he returned to New

York and thought he'd lied to her, it would hurt her. And that didn't sit right with him.

He never wanted her to hurt.

The more time he spent with her, the more important that was becoming.

The more important Harper was.

Daniel liked so much about her. He liked her body and the way she cried out his name when she orgasmed. He liked the way she played with her food and reorganized it on her plate before eating. He liked the tropical vanilla scent she spread on her legs every morning.

Daniel thought having a woman in his world all the time would be irritating.

Harper had left some items in his bathroom this morning and instead of feeling annoyed, he'd stood brushing his teeth, staring at them, wishing they would stay right where they were. Because it meant Harper would be with them.

Then he'd stared at himself in the mirror looking for signs of an alien takeover. Because this was not him. Ever.

And yet, it was with Harper.

So, Daniel had invited her on a date. He planned to enjoy every last minute he had with her and show her how much she meant to him.

Daniel had resources to make a woman feel special, and he was pulling out the big guns tonight to do just that. He hoped she would love it.

"No. I told you, it's a surprise," he said. "Have you got a jacket?"

"Just a little cardigan."

Daniel looked at the tiny piece of clothing, shook his head, and took her hand. "Come with me."

"We're in Hawaii. I don't think I'm going to need a jacket."

She would for this.

Inside his wardrobe, he pulled out a Hugo Boss black bomber jacket. He held up the Ralph Lauren navy jacket he had tucked under his arm, working out which one would swamp her less.

"This one," she said, taking the navy one from his arm. "Not that I will need it."

He leaned in and kissed her. "Let's go."

Instead of going down in the lift, he pressed the button for the top floor, and she stared at him in question. He stared forward, forcing the smile from his face.

The familiar bar and pool area came into view and Daniel knew what Harper was thinking, and she was wrong. He took her hand and led her to another door, up a set of stairs and out onto another area of the roof.

It was barren and dirty.

Daniel quickly glanced at his watch.

"Well, this looks super romantic. You shouldn't have," Harper teased.

"Only the best for you." Daniel lowered his lips to hers and grinned. Then he heard the sound.

Chop, chop, chop.

She gasped against his lips, and he grinned wider.

The helicopter landed as they both held onto their belongings, Harper's hair slashing his face. He pressed down on her back, and they ran into the body of the craft. In moments, they were buckled in, and their headsets were on so they could communicate.

"Oh my God, I love choppers," Harper said, taking his hand. Daniel squeezed it. "Where are we going? Tell me!"

When he just winked at her, she groaned.

An hour later, they landed on the helipad at the *Four Seasons Resort* in Maui.

Harper's nose had been stuck to the window as they neared the island and he'd listen to her chatter over the headphones, feeling so fucking proud he had made her so happy.

They were greeted by the manager, who shook Daniel's hand, knowing exactly who he was, and led them to a private beach dining area. Three staff stood on the edges and discretely seated them, provided them with plumeria leis and poured them a glass of champagne.

"This is incredible," Harper said.

"Happy?" he asked, while their candles were lit.

The sun was setting directly in front of them in a haze of orange and pinks so bright it looked like something from a postcard.

Thank you, Mother Nature. The sunset Daniel hadn't been able to plan, but this was Hawaii, and you were nearly always guaranteed a beautiful burning sky.

"Miserable," Harper replied, looking at him like a woman falling in love. He'd be lying if he said he hated it. "Worst date ever."

"Good," he said and took her hand before he said something he wasn't ready to say.

Probably ever.

For the next few hours, they talked and teased each other as a four-course meal was served, then they headed down onto the sand.

Harper took off her shoes and walked through the surf, holding her pink sundress in a bunch up by her thigh, showing off her toned, sexy legs. Her hair flapped behind them in the breeze.

Daniel walked backwards, watching her, and she smiled at him.

"You're nicer than I thought you'd be."

"I'm only nice to you," he replied, and it was mostly true.

"Rubbish. The way you talk about your brothers, I can tell you love them."

"Yes, but I'm not nice to them. They're little shits," he said, grinning.

"Those *little shits* are directors in your business."

He shrugged. "It's their business as much as it is mine."

"What are they like?" she asked, and Daniel looked out across the ocean. He wanted to answer, but a part of him needed to keep a boundary up. Harper was his in Hawaii.

Nowhere else.

It had to be like this.

"Annoying," he said and stopped walking, so she crashed into him. He took her mouth and kissed her hungrily.

"It's so beautiful here," she said. "Thank you."

"The only thing beautiful is you," Daniel replied.

"Hey, drop the charm. You know I'm a sure thing."

Daniel laughed and swooped her off her feet, loving the little squeal she let out, and carried her up the sand. He dropped her down onto a grassy spot and crouched in front of her.

"Harper. I need to tell you something," Daniel said, going serious.

Her face dropped. "What?"

"I apologize in advance for this, so please don't be angry with me."

"Apologize…what?"

"I don't have a cousin," Daniel said, then shrugged. "Well, I do. Sam. He's a twenty-three-year-old stockbroker."

He'd forgotten about Sam when they had been shopping. Daniel waved his hand in the air all *anyway*…

"A stockbroker? Oh, the gift?" Harper said, the dots finally connecting, and then she frowned.

He hoped she would forgive the little white lie as he reached into the pocket of his pants and pulled out the Cartier watch. His eyes darting between her face and wrist, he gently put it on her.

Harper stared at it; her mouth parted.

"It's insured," Daniel said, keeping her hand in his. "I bought it for you, Harper. It's yours. To remember our time together. Terrible pun, not intended."

Harper's wet eyes met his.

His heart thumped.

"Don't say you won't take it, because I'll throw it in the trash if you do."

She gasped as he knew she would.

"Daniel," she whispered in a growl.

He meant it—if this woman wouldn't wear it, he didn't want it.

Harper took her hand from his and touched it tentatively, moving it around on her arm.

"It's just a gift," he said, shifting on his other foot while crouching in front of her.

"A big gift," she said as he dropped to the sand beside her.

"I wanted to get you something you'd love. That would last a long time."

Because this can't.

Then he saw tears build in her eyes.

"It wasn't meant to make you cry, dammit," Daniel said, pulling her into his arms.

She wrapped herself around him, apologizing into his chest. "Sorry. It was very nice of you. Thank you." She sniffed. "I will love it forever."

He took her chin.

The words were on the tip of his tongue.

Fuck it. He was going to say it.

"Harper, if I could, I would love *you* forever."

A big fat tear dropped down her cheek.

CHAPTER TWENTY

Harper climbed out of bed and slipped into the bathroom. She had no idea what time it was, nor where her handbag had ended up.

When they had returned home to Daniel's penthouse—they took turns at staying in each other's rooms—they had been quick to fall into bed.

As Daniel slept quietly, she tiptoed out into the kitchen area, looking for a bottle of water. All this champagne she'd been having was dehydrating her. She was going to make a point of having some alcohol-free days.

Fortunately, today she wasn't meeting with *BookFlix* until after lunch, and then tomorrow morning the team was flying home to California. That meant she could spend more time with Daniel if he wasn't working.

What's the damn time?

She saw Daniel's phone on the table and walked up to it. One press of the button and his screen would light up, telling her the time. She just wanted to know how much more time she had to sleep or whether to wake him and enjoy more of his body. Like him, she just couldn't get enough.

Harper clicked the button on the side of the iPhone and saw it was five in the morning.

He also had a text message.

She tried really hard not to look at it, but one word jumped off the screen and struck her right in the chest.

Then her heart.

It was from Johnathan Dufort, Daniel's father.

Your engagement announcement is tentatively set for the 25 February.

Engagement. What the fuck? Daniel was engaged?

Nausea rose in her throat, and she went running into the bathroom, reaching the toilet just in time. She threw up.

Daniel was engaged?

She'd been sharing a bed, and every other surface in the penthouse, with another woman's fiancé.

His words came crashing back.

"Harper, if I could, I would love you forever."

She hadn't understood them last night, but now it made total sense.

"Are you okay?" Daniel said from behind her, and she felt his hand on her back. Harper wiped her mouth, flushed the toilet, and stood up. She was shaking.

"Are you sick?" he asked, rubbing his face to wake up.

She could barely make him out in the dim light, but she knew he was the most gorgeous man she'd ever seen.

And he'd lied to her.

She had opened her heart—like a fool again—and let him in. Only to be played.

Again.

She began to wheeze as her chest tightened in anger and pain. "I have to go. Where's my stuff?" She slammed on the lights and they both blinked and squinted, but Harper didn't wait.

She ran from room to room finding her bra, dress, shoes, bags, phone.

"Harper. Stop," he demanded. "What the hell is going on?"

She whirled on him. "No, Daniel. You fucking stop. You fucking stop all of this!"

He stared at her, all color draining from his face.

"What is this about?" His voice was dark.

She pointed out into the living room. "As if you don't know. Go check your phone."

She dressed while Daniel walked out of the room. He never returned. Harper walked past him as he stood staring at the phone, rubbing his face.

"Do not contact me again," she said coldly, then walked out, wishing she could slam the fucking door.

Unfortunately, stupid hotel rooms didn't allow you to do that, so she slapped her handbag uselessly against it and burst into tears.

CHAPTER TWENTY-ONE

Daniel sat staring at his phone for about an hour after Harper had stormed out.

Fury unlike he'd ever experienced ran through his blood and yet all he could do was sit and stare.

He'd lost Harper.

He knew she'd never forgive him, and he couldn't tell her what was going on. He couldn't tell anyone what was happening with the Mackenzie extortion. So there was nothing he could say to make this better.

Fucking nothing.

Eventually, Daniel had fallen asleep with his head lolled back on the sofa. Now he had a throbbing head and a dry throat.

What a fuckup.

He hated the senator more now that his actions had hurt Harper. Fuck the blackmail and fuck the extortion.

He was mad at Harper for not letting him explain, and mad with himself for not saying anything. But there was nothing he could say.

He was the CEO and owner of a billion-dollar business, and they were being extorted. It wasn't something he could share with some girl he met in Hawaii.

Whether he wanted to admit it, that *was* all Harper was.

He had to put his feelings aside and start being responsible. He had thousands of employees around the world who relied on him running this organization and ensuring they thrived. Unless Black Hawke Security found a loophole for them, Daniel would marry the Senator's daughter.

Harper would return to her life. Hate him. They'd miss each other, then forget each other.

Right?

Except that wasn't how it felt. He'd hurt her. And that hurt him. But Daniel couldn't blame anyone else but himself.

Well, except fucking Mackenzie.

Fuck!

He couldn't just leave the islands without talking to Harper. Somehow, he had to tell her as much of the truth as he could without putting the Dufort Dynasty at risk.

He knew Harper well enough to know she'd be very upset and wouldn't speak to him. But Daniel wasn't above using evil tactics to reach her.

Daniel stepped into the conference room minutes before four o'clock.

"Good afternoon, everyone," he said, nodding to all the *BookFlix* faces. "I'm sorry for the intrusion. Ms. Kāne, do you mind if I have a word?"

Harper glared at him, and he noticed her slightly pink eyes. He clenched his jaw, wanting to punch the damn wall.

"Actually, we are just in the middle of wrapping up. Can we speak later?"

Which loosely translated to *over your dead body, asshole.* He'd seen the look before.

"No. This is urgent," he said, using his CEO voice.

Harper glared at him. The room went silent around them. She swallowed and stood. "Well. If you will excuse me, please," she said, collecting her laptop and bag.

"Let's wrap up. We can finish these last pieces on the plane," Denise said, and he gave the woman a smile.

Harper glared at him as he led her to a side room and locked the door.

"What do you want?" she hissed, turning to him.

"I want five minutes to explain."

She rolled her eyes. "You are a man. You're a lying asshole. There is nothing more to know." Harper began to leave.

He grabbed her arm and stopped her.

"Seriously?" she hissed, glaring at her arm.

"Five fucking minutes, Harper." He let go of her arm and saw the flicker of hurt underneath her anger.

"I'm not engaged," Daniel said, getting straight to the point. "I haven't been engaged, nor am I engaged right now. Nor was I before. Is that clear enough? No wife. No fiancée."

It was true.

Daniel *wasn't* engaged at this very moment, and he hoped to God he wouldn't be.

"I doubt I'm even husband material. In fact, I know I'm not," he said.

"Then why does dear old daddy think you are? I saw the text, Daniel," Harper snapped.

Daniel really wanted to lie—to say something to ease her pain and allow things to return to the way they were.

But he couldn't.

And he couldn't tell Harper the complete truth, which left him in a tricky position. So he found a middle ground, which was as close to the truth as possible.

"My father wants me to marry a woman in New York," he said, taking a step closer to her. "It's a business decision. Nothing to do with love. I have no interest in her and certainly don't want to marry her."

Harper stared back at him, and he saw the ice melting a little. Her eyes darted around his face until they met his.

"I can't do this," she whispered. "I'm sorry. I thought I could but…"

He nodded. "I understand."

Did he really think Harper was going to bounce back and throw her arms around him? No.

Okay, yes.

But that wasn't why he was here. He had wanted to ease the pain he had caused her and was hoping she would hate him just a little less to knowing some of the truth.

"It was important to me, you knew. I swear I was single the day I met you. Just as I am now."

Harper nodded and glanced away. "Thank you for telling me."

His chest tightened and a kind of panic began to set in. He wanted to drag her upstairs and never let her go.

Fucking hell.

She was never meant to be this important.

Right now, he was fighting the urge to pull her into his arms and tell Harper *she* was the woman he wanted to love and spend his life with.

Daniel shook his head.

He couldn't.

Ensuring the Dufort Dynasty was protected had to come first. For his father, his family, the thousands of people who worked for them. For his future.

Anyway, what the hell did he know about love? He'd sworn off it as much as Harper had. Neither of them trusted it or wanted a marriage.

Without the latter, and the visa it would secure, Harper could never live in America. Which meant they couldn't even date casually and see how things went.

A long-distance relationship between New Zealand and New York was as far away as one could get. Even with his financial means. It was a hell of a long way and they both knew it.

Hello reality.

He smiled sadly at her.

She did the same.

"I'm sorry," Daniel said.

"I know." Then Harper surprised him and slipped into his arms.

They stood holding each other like they were on a sinking ship. And it fucking felt like it.

CHAPTER TWENTY-TWO

Two days later, Harper's tears had nearly dried up. She missed Daniel more than she should have for someone she had only known a week. She spent far too much time checking her texts and lying to herself about it.

The *BookFlix* team had left yesterday afternoon, so she had Facetimed Kristen and burst into tears, telling her everything.

Harper had planned to change her flights and return home, but Kris had talked her out of it, reminding her she was in *Fucking Hawaii, girlfriend.*

Despite everything, Harper had smiled.

"Yeah. You're right."

"Don't let a dumb boy ruin everything. This is an exciting moment in your career." Kristen had said. "Do you know how many authors would love to be in your shoes right now?"

Harper had nodded humbly.

She knew how fortunate she was. *Very.* But they were different things. Being grateful for her career was one thing. Falling for the wrong man—again— was quite the other. Clearly, she was not designed for casual relationships. She'd probably fall in love with a tree if it hugged her back.

"Dig out your holiday list and get focused," Kristen instructed her. "It's nice he apologized and maybe he is, or maybe he isn't, marrying this chick, but you don't want to get tied up in all that rich folk stuff."

Harper had snorted. "Rich folk stuff?"

Kristen had shrugged. "Yeah, you know, they marry each other to build their fortunes. It's super creepy. No love involved."

Harper's eyes glazed over as she recalled what Daniel had said about his father wanting the marriage to go ahead. What must it feel like to be forced into these things?

For a moment, she felt sorry for him. Then she felt something shift within her.

"You know, Kris, I have no right being this hurt and upset. He never promised me anything," Harper said, frowning. "Nor did I ask for anything. We simply fell into this holiday romance, and things got really intense."

"So, what are you saying?"

Harper sighed.

"Perhaps I overreacted. If he was engaged, it would have made him a complete asshole, but when I gave him the opportunity to explain, and he told me he wasn't and isn't, I could have let it go," she said. "I mean, his father *is* trying to coerce him. That's not his fault."

"But—"

Harper interrupted her. "I'm not saying I'm going to jump back in, but I don't need to be so mad.

You know? Whatever is going on in New York is none of my business. Daniel hasn't cheated on anyone, least of all me."

Kristen shrugged and nodded. "All of that is true."

"I just don't want to walk around mad at life anymore. I did enough of that with David."

If she was being honest with herself, the time she'd spent with Daniel was the most romantic and wonderful days and nights she'd ever experienced. He'd been funny, respectful, protective, and deliciously possessive. The sex, intoxicating.

Harper would not regret it for another day.

The only regret she *did* have was that Daniel wouldn't be the man she'd spent the rest of her life with.

And she'd had no idea she had even felt like that about him. Or perhaps she did, but she was trying to ignore it.

No matter how she looked at it, they were always going to part ways.

Harper bunched her lips.

"You know he's probably a pain in the ass to live with in real life," she said, letting out a little laugh. "Like, he probably leaves the toilet seat up and scrunches the toothpaste tube."

Kristen nodded and failed badly at hiding the pity from her face. "Babes, were you actually thinking it would be something real?"

"No, no. Of course not," Harper replied, talking faster. "You know how these things get confusing when you're in them. Sex messes with your brain. Especially when it's that good."

"Okay, honey, well, I'm glad you are feeling better about this now."

They talked for a little while longer, Kristen reminding her to call her mom. Apparently, she'd been texting poor Kris when Harper hadn't replied.

She didn't want to speak to her right now. The woman was like a dog with a bone if she thought someone had a broken heart. Plus, Harper didn't want her mother knowing anything about Daniel.

By morning, Harper had decided to do a group island tour, which would take her out of Waikiki for the day. She phoned down really early and got the last seat on the Circle Island Tour, which left at 8:00 a.m.

Dressed in a pair of denim cutoffs, Converse sneakers, a cropped black bra-top and a white loose shirt, Harper stood outside the hotel along with a handful of tourists waiting for their bus.

She pulled her hair up in a ponytail and slipped on a ball cap and pair of glasses.

"Is this the Circle Tour?" a guy beside her asked. He was rubbing his face, and she spotted his two friends wearing dark glasses. Clearly, they'd all had a late night.

"Yes," she said, grinning. "Sore head?"

"The worst, and someone forgot to get the Tylenol," he said, glaring at his friend.

Harper let out a small laugh.

"Here," she said, digging out a small bottle she always carried with her. When you suffered from period pain like she had all her life, you never left home without it.

All three of the men looked at her like she was Mother Teresa, which just made her laugh more.

Bottles of water were twisted open, and they downed the capsules, letting out a sigh.

"You're a lifesaver," the first guy said. "I'm Cooper. This is Graydon and Luke."

They looked close to her age and a lot of fun. Cheeky, but fun. "Hey. I'm Harper."

"You on your own? In Hawaii?" Cooper asked.

Harper nodded. "Kind of. I've been here on business and...with a friend. Who is, well, he's gone."

Cooper smirked at her. "Break up?"

She shook her head and waved her hand out. "No. Not like that."

"Well, Harper," Cooper said, slinging an arm over her shoulder playfully. "Stick with us and we'll look after you."

"And kick the guy's ass if he needs kicking," Graydon said, nodding.

Harper laughed. "Thanks, guys."

"Hands off, Coop. I'm sure Harper is far more interested in a computer scientist from LA than a boring old neuroscientist," Luke said, winking at her.

"Oh, boy. This is going to be a long day." She laughed and all three of them grinned.

When the bus arrived, they all piled in and the three men did *rock, paper, scissors* to decide who would sit next to her, while she shook her head in embarrassment. By this point, they had the attention of the other passengers.

Cooper won, and gave his friends the bird, plopping down on the seat next to her, then winked at her.

Ten minutes later, all three of them were asleep.

They woke up when they arrived at the macadamia farm and stood guzzling coffee while Harper browsed and purchased a few touristy things.

Then they stopped for lunch in Haleiwa on the north shore after kayaking, where they spotted some turtles on the beach. On the way back across the island, there was one more stop.

Dole Plantation.

After the tour, they sat outside with an ice-cold pineapple whip.

"God, it's hot," Luke said, stretching out his legs.

"I think it's worse when you have a hangover," Graydon said.

Harper nodded. "I agree."

"So, what business are you doing here?" Cooper asked.

Harper had already shared she was from New Zealand and was an author. Women's fiction was all she'd said, as telling men she wrote steamy romance usually gave the wrong impression.

It amused her how people thought romance authors were literally their characters, but no one went around accusing Stephen King of being an axe murderer.

"Just book stuff," she replied. "What about you guys?"

"I've just completed my PhD in *boring old neuroscience*," Cooper said, mocking Luke's earlier comment. "We all met at Harvard."

"We graduated earlier than Brainiac here," Graydon said, nudging Cooper.

"What did you study?" she asked him.

"I did my master's in architecture," he replied.

"That's awesome."

"Hmmm," Graydon said, shrugging. "My father doesn't think so. He's a property investor and wanted me to work alongside him, not do the, and I quote, *fancy design shit.*"

"Ouch," Harper said. "That's a little ignorant, don't you think? Without the design, well, it's just a roof and walls."

"Exactly," Graydon said. "But yeah, he's tolerated it while I did the degree, but now we'll see."

Harper frowned. "I don't understand. Why is it his decision?"

Luke leaned forward. "These two are trust-fund babies. Their lives are not their own."

"Shut it," Cooper said, throwing something at him. "You're hardly living on the streets, *rich boy.*"

Luke laughed.

"Now, tell us about this douchebag," Cooper said, changing the subject, and Harper flinched.

"Dude," Luke growled at Cooper.

"No. It's not like that," Harper said, but she didn't know what it *was* like. Or what she could say.

"Was he your boyfriend?" Graydon asked.

Harper shook her head. The last thing she wanted to do was tell them she had been involved with a guy on the island and…well, she just didn't want them to think she was some easy girl.

"It just didn't work out," she said. "No big deal. That's life, right?"

The three of them nodded and regaled her with tales of their own relationship failures. Many of which were hilarious and had her laughing.

"I'm not kidding you. She actually moved into my apartment before I got home," Luke said. "I had only given her the key the day before."

Harper finished her pineapple whip and dropped it onto the table. "Wow, that *is* kind of psycho."

"We warned him she was cray, but he was obsessed with her boobs," Cooper said, shrugging.

Harper turned to the blonde, who looked like he belonged in Hawaii. "Seriously, is that what it comes down to with men? Boobs and stuff? Don't you care about conversation or whether someone squeezes the toothpaste tube the right way?"

"Umm," Cooper said, glancing at his friends for help. "I guess toothpaste is important. How do you do it?"

She let out a little laugh. "The right way, of course, but I meant as an example. Ignore me. I'm just off men. Except you three, of course."

Graydon jumped up, surprising them all.

"Hey. Tomorrow is Valentine's Day. We can take you to the party and be your dates. All three of us—your ex be dammed."

Oh God.

How had she forgotten it was Valentine's Day? Worst day of the damn year. Ugh.

Wait. What party?

She watched all three of the guy's nod and high five each other.

"Is he still in Hawaii? At the hotel? We'll totally make him jealous," Cooper said.

Harper shook her head. "It's not like that. What party?"

"The Dufort Valentine's Day party. The signs in the lifts—didn't you see them?"

Harper shook her head.

"Red, black and white dress code," Luke said. "It's at the rooftop *Altitude* bar."

"I'm not sure…"

"You're going. It's final," Graydon said as he shot their empty cups into the trash can as if they were basketballs. "*And yes!*" he said when the last one made it.

Harper shook her head and laughed.

They made her laugh. They were funny and good company. So far, despite their joking around, none of them had crossed the friendship line, and she quite liked their desire to defend her. It made her feel protected when she'd spent the last few days feeling raw and sad.

Perhaps it would be fun.

It was unlikely the event was Daniel's style, so she couldn't see him attending, if he was even still in Hawaii. For all she knew, he was back in New York.

Harper nodded.

"Okay, I'll go."

CHAPTER TWENTY-THREE

"If we do this, there's no going back," Josh Hawke said.

Daniel tapped his fingers on the table. Finally, he'd received a call back from them with some information. Unfortunately, the news wasn't great. They had nothing to use that would help with the blackmail.

So they were stepping things up to another level.

"No, there isn't," Daniel said.

Josh was right. It was a big fucking deal to wire a senator's office. But then again, it was a big fucking deal to extort the CEO of a hotel dynasty into marrying your daughter, and Daniel was not in a merciful or law-abiding mood.

Not after what he'd seen this morning.

He'd gone for an early morning run along Waikiki, past the aquarium and up to Diamond Head—only the entrance, not the top—and back. Cooling down, he'd walked the last few blocks. When he'd neared the entrance to the hotel, Daniel had seen a man standing with a woman. He had his arm around her shoulders and was grinning down at her.

The woman was laughing.

His woman.

Harper may have been in a hat and sunglasses, but he knew her body. Inside and out.

Every fucking inch of it.

Daniel's fists had clenched, and his blood boiled as he watched the man, and his two friends vie for Harper's attention.

It had been three days.

Three fucking days.

Not that she owed him anything. Harper was fucking gorgeous—what did he think was going to happen? That she'd walk around Hawaii crying over him?

Fuck. Yeah, he had.

God, he was an asshole.

She had every right to enjoy her holiday and be with whoever she wanted.

Daniel didn't have to be happy about it, though, and he wasn't. Five times he'd picked up his phone to text her. And say what?

I'm sorry, I think I'm in love with you. But oh yeah, I can't be with you, anyway.

So he'd punched the living fuck out of his boxing bag for starters and messaged Josh, saying they needed to talk.

Unless he could get some evidence, there was foul play here, and unless he married this fucking woman, the Dufort Dynasty was in financial jeopardy. They would lose board members. Their shares would drop, and it could mean selling properties.

He would not let that happen.

So that left marrying Nadia fucking Mackenzie for five years. Then he would be free.

But he'd lose Harper.

No, he'd already lost Harper. Hadn't he?

And is that what he wanted? Harper. In his life. In New York.

Jesus.

Was he serious about her?

Or the better question was, could he live without her? Could he live with other men, putting their arms around her? Their mouths on her?

Fuck. He needed to punch someone.

"There's talk. He's making a run for president," Josh said. "It could take us time to get proof, but I think this blackmail is about funding his campaign."

And yeah, it would do that, but only if they paid out.

"So he's expecting Dufort Hotels to pay, and not go through with the wedding," Daniel stated.

"I think so." Josh replied. "I can't be sure, but I think the Senator believes you would be so against the idea of marriage you would pay out the cash."

Mother fucker.

"Let's proceed," Daniel said. "I need some God damn information against this asshole. But fuck, Josh, don't get caught."

There was silence and he silently kicked himself. It was unlikely he'd offended the man, but it was a dick thing to say. The private security agency owner was, after all, one of the best.

"We're good, Dufort," Josh said, then added more darkly, "If Mackenzie's guilty, I won't let him get away with this. Nor will he ever become my president."

Daniel felt a shiver run through his body. He had a feeling if Josh decided on something, even someone like the powerful senator wouldn't have a chance.

"Gotcha."

"It just might not be as quick as you want. Ask for a long engagement or some shit."

Daniel shook his head at the reality of the situation. "Yeah. Fuck."

"I'll be in touch when we get something."

They ended the call and Daniel leaned back in his chair, running his hands through his hair.

"Fuck!!!!" he yelled, slamming his fist on the table.

Time was running out.

He didn't have long before Mackenzie was sending the engagement notice out. Which meant he had to approve the fucking prenup his lawyers had drafted.

He dialed the man's number.

"Hello, Daniel," Duke Johnson said upon answering.

"I'm sending through the changes," he growled. "Add in a clause that Nadia can't use the Dufort name. Then it's approved."

"Got it," he replied. "I'll have it for you in the morning, Hawaii time."

Daniel ended the call and tossed the phone on the table, cursing again.

Fucking Mackenzie.

No one fucked with the Dufort's—they were a powerful family.

Many of the senators and governors were, in one way or another, in their pockets. They weren't a corrupt family, but it helped to get legislation passed when you wanted to build hotels or change laws restricting progress. It was how business and politics were done.

It was no different from other countries around the world. Daniel had dined with world leaders, Prime Ministers, and royals to influence their decisions many times.

Now, this asshole had them over a barrel because of a lost document.

Fuck.

Or rather, a stolen document. Because how the hell did it just disappear?

It didn't.

Someone fucking took it. There had to be someone on the inside. Who would have access to or a connection with Mackenzie to do this? Someone desperate for some cash? Usually, it was money that made people do bad things.

He pressed a button on his phone, and it dialed.

"Daniel."

"Hunter," he said to his brother. "I need your help, buddy."

"You, okay?" Hunter asked, and Daniel calmed just hearing his brother's voice.

"I'm working an angle, but I need to step things up. I'm not going down without a fight."

"About fucking time."

Daniel updated him on the situation and asked him to sniff around and find out who might have financial difficulties or have a gripe with Dufort Dynasty.

"They'll need to have access to the finance or legal team areas and files."

"As far as I know, only Brent, Suzanne and anyone with Dufort in their name have access to those vaults," Hunter said. "I'll dig around and find out what I can."

"Codes get given out. Just be discrete. I don't want to raise any alarms. This is already a tenuous situation."

"Of course," Hunter said. "We'll work this out. You're not marrying that asshole's daughter."

No. He fucking wasn't.

Daniel ended the call and walked into the bedroom.

He should head back to New York. Things were turning to shit. None of the meetings he'd scheduled in Hawaii were as important as this, and frankly, he was distracted wondering what Harper was up to.

He should leave.

The last thing he wanted was to bump into Harper and her harem of horny young men. He was likely to knock one of their heads off.

Or kidnap her and take her home with him.

Jesus.

Could he really leave Hawaii and not see her again?

The answer was no.

CHAPTER TWENTY-FOUR

Harper bolted upright and let out a scream.

She blinked, looking around, and saw she was in her hotel suite in Hawaii.

Slowly, she got her bearings.

Wow, what the hell was that?

A nightmare.

About Daniel.

He had flown home and his plane had crashed. His private jet. She didn't even know if he had a private jet or flew commercial. But vividly she could see the flames and his face screaming her name.

Harper was covered in sweat.

She reached over and pulled a handful of tissues out of the box and patted her face and chest. She was going to need a shower.

Suddenly, she heard banging on her door.

"Harper! Open up! Harper!"

Daniel?

She ran to the door and pulled it open.

"What's going on?" she asked, her eyes wide at the man standing there in only a pair of boxers.

He pushed into her room, grabbing her arms, and looking over her like she was the one who had been in the plane crash.

"Are you okay?"

Harper took in his large, muscular chest and six-pack abs and nodded.

"Up here, sunshine," he said, taking her chin. "What happened?"

She shook her head and stepped away.

"I had a nightmare. Did you hear me from all the way down the hall?"

Daniel stepped over to the ranch slider and pulled them shut. "You left these open. Sound travels at this time in the morning."

Harper looked at the clock on the wall. It was only 3:00 a.m.

"Sorry. I didn't mean to wake you."

"Don't apologize. Fuck, Harper. I was worried. You screamed like someone was trying to kill you."

She looked down at the barely there night dress she wore and back at him.

"Don't do that," Daniel said, shaking his head. "I've seen every inch of you. I've *touched* every inch of you."

Harper moved to the sofa and sat down, pulling a thin throw over her despite the heat. Daniel frowned and sat down in a chair opposite her.

"You want to tell me what the dream was about?"

"Not really," she said.

"Do you want a glass of water?"

She nodded, and he returned a minute later with a cold glass from the fridge. This time, he sat beside her. He watched her drink it and place it on the small table beside her.

"Can I please fucking hug you? My heart is still racing," he said, rubbing his hand over his face.

Harper launched herself into his arms, promising to hate herself for it tomorrow. For now, she just needed Daniel's arms around her.

He moaned into her hair and kissed her head. Neither of them said anything, and she began to doze. Soon she felt him rearrange them on the sofa, so they were lying down, and wrap her up in his arms.

The next thing, Harper woke up to the heat of the Hawaii sun pouring over her.

Daniel was gone.

Happy damn Valentine's Day.

A few hours later, Harper was back with the three amigos, as she'd nicknamed them. They were out shopping in Waikiki for outfits for the Valentine's Day party tonight.

When she'd met them in the foyer, they had surprised her with gifts of heart-shaped chocolates and a beautiful bunch of red roses. And three kisses on her cheek.

She had blushed.

"Thank you. Oh my God, you are all so sweet." Then she'd handed the gifts to a concierge who had taken them to her suite, so they could go shopping.

Now, walking down Kalakaua Avenue with the three tall men, Harper felt like she had a personal security entourage.

"We need to find you some dates," Harper said. "You can't hang around me all evening."

"Oh, don't worry, I have my eye on the blonde from room 2506," Luke said, grinning. "She said she'd be there."

Harper smiled.

"What about you?" she said, nudging Cooper.

"Nope, I only have eyes for you, my darling," he said, looping his arm over her shoulders. He was doing that a lot lately, and Harper was starting to think he had a crush on her.

Harper glanced at him, and he winked back at her, but this time there was a warmth in it as his eyes lingered too long. She didn't want to encourage him. After being back in Daniel's arms last night, she could not lie to herself anymore.

She was in love with Daniel Dufort.

Rightly or wrongly.

It changed nothing. She was still going home in a few days. He was still returning to New York and maybe marrying the woman his father had lined up for him, but that was how she felt, and it was going to take time to get over him.

The odd thing about it all was Harper couldn't imagine Daniel just lying down and accepting being manipulated. He'd told her how he felt about marriage after seeing his parents break up. Perhaps Kristen was right. Rich people married for business connections and convenience.

Maybe there was something in it for him financially.

The thought made her even more sad.

Had their connection meant nothing to Daniel? *"Harper, if I could, I would love you forever."* For a man with so much power, he seemed to be giving it away to other people pretty easily.

Or she wasn't as important to him as he had said.

The right thing for her to do was let him go, and definitely not jump into anything else for a long time. She needed to be single and just focus on her career.

Harper did like Cooper.

Under different circumstances, she possibly could have feelings for him if she hadn't had met Daniel. Cooper was cheeky and very attractive. He stood at least six-foot-two and was very well built. With all his gorgeous blonde hair, Cooper looked like a wealthy local, though she had yet to see him on a surfboard.

But she had met Daniel and her heart belonged to him.

For now.

They stopped at the *Volcom* store where the guys found black and white Hawaiian shirts. They got one each.

"Harpster, we need to find you a red dress," Luke said. "Then we'll match the theme of the party."

Harpster?

Cooper caught her eye, and they laughed.

"Okay, fine. Follow me." She laughed and led them to Macys where she found a Tommy Bahama's halter dress in dark red.

Graydon whistled when she stepped out of the changing rooms. He was leaning against the wall, his arms crossed and shaking his head. Cooper punched him in the arm and Graydon laughed while he wobbled, then caught his balance.

"That back, though. *Jesus*," Cooper said, and she turned and took in the low, almost non-existent back of the dress in the mirror. It finished just above her panty line.

"Too much?" she asked, and all three men shook their heads with a resounding *nooo*.

She giggled. They were so good for her ego.

Harper paid for the dress, and the three of them walked across the road and sat on the beach, eating lunch on the sand.

"We're going to fit in a workout before the party," Cooper said, handing his trash to Luke, who tossed it in the trash can. "You coming back or staying here?"

Harper looked around the beach and felt the calm seep into her bones.

"I'm just going to stay here and wander around some more," she said. "I'll see you guys in the foyer at 5:00 p.m."

Graydon stood and did some playful punches with Luke, while Cooper leaned in and kissed her cheek. She blushed, and he gave her another of his winks. "See you then, Kiwi."

"Okay."

As she watched them walk away, Harper chewed the inside of her cheek. She didn't want to say anything to Cooper in front of his friends, but tonight she would take him aside and let him know she wasn't interested in taking their friendship to a different level.

She loved hanging out with them, and had a soft spot for Cooper, but she didn't want to lead him on.

Harper kicked off her shoes and used her bag as a pillow, lying down on the warm sand. She stared up at the bright blue sky and thought about her life.

She would be back here later in the year for the media launch of her stories as a tv series. Or sooner if she and Kristen did a girls' weekend mid-year to get away from New Zealand's winter.

By then, her life would be about to change.

Her books, because of *BookFlix,* would be in the global spotlight. And that included her as an author.

Harper really did not know how it would impact her day-to-day life, but she was excited.

Or at least, once she stopped feeling so sad about Daniel, she would be.

Who hadn't text.

Or called.

Or even left a note.

He'd simply disappeared at some point this morning after Harper had fallen asleep.

And that hurt.

Later than night, Harper stepped out into the foyer feeling pretty good, considering everything. She'd had a long soak in the enormous spa bath in her penthouse and paired her new Michael Kors black heels with her red dress.

They weren't Manolo Blahnik like the women Daniel dated wore, but she doubted he'd be here tonight, anyway. If he was, he'd see she was wearing his watch.

The Cartier.

She looked up and saw her three amigos. They hadn't spotted her yet. She grinned at how they had all styled their matching shirts differently. Cooper was wearing a pair of blue jeans that hugged his very nice butt. Graydon, a pair of long black shorts, and Luke, a pair of tan cargo shorts.

For a bunch of *trust-fund babies,* as Luke had called them, they were a lot of fun and very down to earth.

Cooper turned first and a smile lit up his face.

Harper blushed.

"Hell, yes," Graydon said and took the lead in walking across the floor to lean down and kiss her cheek. "You look gorgeous."

"Thank you," she said, as Luke and Cooper followed suit. "You guys scrub up pretty well yourselves."

Cooper offered her his arm. "Come, milady, delicious beverages await us."

The four of them rode the lift to *Altitude* which was decorated in red, black, and white everything as per the Valentine's theme.

They were handed red and white leis and a red cocktail as they walked in.

Harper smiled up at Cooper, who had put his hand on the small of her back. She was ready to relax and have some fun.

Damn, she deserved it.

They found a table and got settled. A small band was set up in the corner singing cover songs, and the sun was beginning its descent in the sky. Harper loved this time of the day in Hawaii. There was something calm and deliciously happy about the warm tropical air as the sun disappeared.

It felt as if everything was right in the world.

And maybe it would be, if she opened up to different possibilities with a man one day.

Not today, but one day.

She glanced at Cooper, who was laughing at something Luke said. Maybe he was right for her? Or maybe not.

Tonight, she just wanted to have fun.

The party soon heated up, the sun long gone, and a dance floor appeared in front of the band. Grayson pulled Harper onto the dance floor, and it wasn't long before they were all dancing.

For a moment, all her worries disappeared, and she let the music, cocktails, and tropical heat swallow her up.

CHAPTER TWENTY-FIVE

Daniel tucked his phone back in his pocket and lifted his whisky to his lips. Despite the music, he could hear the ice cubes clink against the glass. He let one fall into his mouth and crunched it.

It was hot tonight. Hotter than it usually would be in mid-February, and it was a stark reminder he was still in fucking Hawaii.

Had he prepared the jet for flight this afternoon? *Yes.*

Had he flown?

No.

Daniel knew why. He'd crept out of Harper's room as the sun rose, after holding her all night on her damn uncomfortable sofa.

Leaving just felt wrong.

Then Harry had asked if he was attending the Valentine's party and Daniel had said he was. He told himself he was only going to spend time with his regional staff, but that was a lie.

Obviously.

Was he over with his team enjoying a Mai Tai? Or was he mooching in the shadows, knocking back whisky?

Daniel let out a small groan.

Harper made him think things, feel things, and do things he usually never would. It was infuriating. He wanted to be mad at her, but instead, he was mad at himself.

He should never have let himself get so involved with her.

Right now, she was being twirled around the dance floor by a man who was clearly besotted with her. *Know the feeling, pal.*

He'd been watching them for over an hour and the guy had *lovesick puppy* written all over his face.

If it hadn't been for the fact he knew Harper's body and her reactions, Daniel would probably have strode across the rooftop and punched the guy a good one.

But Daniel knew her. He knew her body. He knew how she reacted and leaned into *his* touch.

He watched Harper fight an internal battle. She liked this man well enough. He was a good-looking man. Tall, muscular, and charming. He had money. Daniel saw it in the way he dressed and held himself.

Yet her body tensed. Her eyes dropped. Her lips pressed together.

Because of Daniel.

Did he feel guilty? Yes.

And no.

He wanted her to be happy. With him. On his arm. In his bed. In his fucking house.

What the hell?

Now he had her living in New York fucking City?

Fucking hell. He should have flown home.

"There you are," Akino said, spotting him as he walked by. "We thought you may have left."

I should have.

Daniel cleared his throat and stood up from the wall. "I nearly did. I will be gone by tomorrow afternoon."

Akino gave him a knowing nod.

They both knew Akino had seen him with Harper over the past few days, and it was obvious he was standing here, watching her like a fucking stalker.

"The team's over here," he said, throwing his thumb over his shoulder. "If you want to say a quick hello, then get back to other things."

Other things.

Like illegally listening in on a US senator?

Like interrogating his staff to find out who was liable to be blackmailed into stealing a document that could cost them over a billion dollars?

Like trying to fix this fuck up so he didn't have to marry a woman he didn't like, let alone love?

Like fighting every instinct in his body to slam his whisky down and punch the man who had his hands on Harper's hips? Fucker was grinning at her like she was his.

She fucking wasn't.

Harper was…

Not his. She couldn't be.

"Sure," he said instead.

"You want something different?" Akino asked, staring at his now empty glass.

"Yeah, why not? A double Mai Tai," he said, nodding, as they stepped up to the group of off-duty Dufort staff. "Evening, folks."

They greeted him with a mix of *Mr. Dufort. Hello, sir*, and shy smiles from the newer team members.

"You've put on a great event. Well done," he said, glancing around—everywhere but the few inches of space Harper took up. "Especially the sunset—that was a nice touch."

Everyone laughed appropriately at his shit joke, and he took the drink from Akino, who had rejoined them.

"It's been great having you back in Hawaii, sir. Hopefully, we'll see you back later in the year for the media launch of Ms. Kāne's show."

For the first time in Daniel's life, he had no idea what his life would look like in a few months.

From the day he'd been born, or at least from the time he could remember, he'd known he was going to college, knew he was getting into Harvard. Knew he would be the chief executive officer of the Dufort Dynasty. He knew his life path and what was expected of him.

Unlike some kids who grew up resenting it, or rebelling against it, Daniel felt it was his destiny. He loved what he did. He was proud of what his father had created, and he felt a strong sense of responsibility to ensure his family and all the employees of Dufort Hotels continued to thrive under his leadership.

And two years into it, they were.

The numbers were up and, ironically, their debt decreasing. Except for the little issue of extortion they were dealing with right now. If he didn't marry Nadia, Dufort would pay out an enormous amount of money.

It would derail the entire organization, so it just wasn't an option.

Daniel nodded and answered questions from his team, who were excited to have him there with them. They took photos and posted them on their social media channels.

There were a few flirty glances, but he deflected them. Daniel had a strict approach to anybody in his company who thought they could get ahead by sleeping with the boss or take advantage of junior staff. In fact, when he'd become CEO, he'd implemented a new company policy which clearly stated there were to be no relationships between staff. Whether for fifteen minutes or longer.

In other words, no fucking your colleagues.

With Harper only fifty feet away, the last thing he wanted her to see was some young Hawaiian employee of his flirting with him.

Holding her in his arms last night had felt different. When he'd first met Harper, it had been pure lust, and yes, she'd been a challenge. Men loved a conquest and Daniel was an alpha. Her disinterest in him, along with her stunning beauty, had been an aphrodisiac. Then, when they'd begun talking and spending time together, something had shifted.

Every kiss. Every time they'd made love, it had felt like he was becoming more and more addicted to her.

Somewhere between that damn hurricane and the moment he'd slipped the Cartier watch onto her wrist, she'd slipped inside his heart.

Thanks to his father, and that fucking text, it had ended far too soon. Fuck it. Daniel didn't know if that had been a blessing or a curse, but if he could change time, he'd throw his phone off the side of the building.

The truth was, he was falling in love with Harper.

Hell, maybe he *was* in love with her.

The fact he was still standing on Hawaiian soil pretty much spoke to that. He seemed incapable of leaving her, and yet, he knew tomorrow afternoon he would have to go.

His chest tightened.

He lifted his eyes and found Harper looking at him. It was quick. Then she smiled at the man she was dancing with, and he twirled her around.

Fast, but not fast enough. Daniel hadn't missed the emotion in those deep blue eyes of hers.

Pain, sadness, hope, and disappointment.

Daniel could take the pain away. He was going to. He had to. For both of them.

Plus, if he had to watch another man touch *his* girl for another minute more, he was going to punch someone.

"Excuse me," he said to Akino, placing his glass on the table.

Akino followed his eyes. "See you on your next visit, Daniel," the man said, using his first name for the first time.

Daniel slapped him on the shoulder. "Keep up the good work, Akino."

Then he went to get his girl.

Because she *was* fucking his.

Harper had never danced so much. It was easier than standing around watching women swoon over Daniel, or continually catching his eyes on her.

He hadn't even bothered to say hello, or text her, after spending the night with her on the sofa.

And why was she bothering to even think about him when she had Cooper, Graydon and Luke, who were treating her like she was a Goddess? Especially Cooper, whom she'd spent most of the night trying to keep some kind of boundary in place with.

A slower song came on, and when the others left, Cooper stayed on the dance floor and pulled her in for a close dance.

"Hey." He smiled, and she'd put money on this good-looking man having broken some hearts in his life. He held her in his arms confidently and moved them around the dance floor.

"Hey, back," she replied, dropping her eyes.

"You look beautiful," Cooper said, ducking his head a little to catch her eye.

"Thank you." Harper smiled. "You guys have been amazing. *You* have been amazing. I'm glad I met you."

His hand rested on the small of her back as they swayed to the song, and his thumb mindlessly moved across her bare back.

Harper was relaxed, but not totally. Her eyes darted to the red decorations and fairy lights twinkling off the pool water. It would have been a truly romantic moment had she not given her heart away to someone else.

For a moment, it made her angry. She liked Cooper. He made her smile. She fit in his arms, and he had a way of making her feel special. Like he would do anything for her.

Cooper was that guy who would never let you down. You'd marry him, have a great sex life, and grow old together, not wanting for anything.

She wanted that.

"It hasn't been entirely selfless. I think you know that." Cooper said, his eyes growing serious.

Harper nodded and bunched her lips. "I know."

"He's here tonight, isn't he?" Cooper asked.

Harper hesitated, then decided she didn't want to lie. Not to Cooper.

"Yes." She nodded and moved in closer, laying her head against his chest. Cooper wrapped his arms around her. "I'm sorry."

He kissed the top of her head.

"Nothing to be sorry about, beautiful. You need to decide what you want. I think you know I want you. I'm not going to just give up—that's not my nature."

She lifted her head and saw the determination in Cooper's eyes.

"We're here until next week, but if you need time, then that's okay. New Zealand isn't that far away."

Harper's eyes moistened.

This man was fighting for her. When had any man done that? Least of all Daniel Dufort. He'd slipped in and stolen her heart, then left when things got difficult.

Why wouldn't he fight for her like Cooper was?

Harper knew the answer. She wasn't his priority. Daniel had responsibilities and expectations on him. She had no place in his world.

She never would.

"Can I interrupt?"

Cooper stilled and turned as Harper looked up into Daniel Dufort's powerful eyes.

Her heart thumped.

Cooper's arms released her as she stared at the man dressed head to toe in black. His shorts fit his large thighs like they were made for him—and probably were—while the black shirt did nothing to hide his large, muscular chest. Tonight, he had a little scruff on his face, and it suited him.

She tried to ignore his icy blue eyes as they bore down on her.

God, he was gorgeous.

The familiar heat blazed between them as Daniel looked at her as if she were the only thing that mattered. If only that were true.

Cooper didn't move away. He remained up against her body, waiting for a response. The choice was hers.

She lifted her eyes apologetically, and he nodded, kissing her cheek. "Remember what I said."

The two men gave each other a respectful nod as Cooper walked away.

Daniel didn't hesitate. He pulled her into his powerful arms with such possessiveness it took her breath away. They were both big men, but Daniel was larger, taller, and his energy far more dominant.

Harper felt dizzy.

A slightly more upbeat song played, but they remained slow dancing.

"I'm leaving tomorrow," Daniel finally said, and she nodded. "God, Harper, I can't stand this."

She lay her head against his chest to hide the tears building. Her sniff gave her away, but Daniel didn't say anything. Instead, his fingers dug into her skin.

"Can we—"

A stronger woman probably would have said no. But she didn't. Harper nodded without hesitation before he'd finished the sentence.

Daniel released her and glanced over at her three amigos. "Do you want to say goodbye?"

Harper watched as Graydon, Cooper and Luke stared at the floor, walls, and sky, pretending to be interested in whatever they saw, when it was obvious, they'd been watching her.

"Give me a minute," she said. "I need to get my purse."

Daniel nodded and plunged his hands into his shorts.

Harper walked over to her friends, looking at them like, *I know I'm fucking up here, I'm fully aware of it, but can we all just pretend I'm making a sensible adult decision and we can deal with it tomorrow?*

"So…" she started.

"Go," Graydon said, making it easy for her.

"We'll be here with the Tylenol tomorrow," Luke said, referencing the first day they'd meet. She gave him a grateful smile and picked up her purse, then turned to Cooper.

"I'm not going to lie, that's some tough competition," he said, after shooting a glance in Daniel's direction. "You didn't mention it was Daniel Dufort."

Harper shook her head, not knowing what to say. She didn't want to feel like she was deciding between them.

"I just have to do this. To say goodbye," she said, then poked him in the abs with her purse. "Come on, I live in New Zealand, Coop. There are a dozen American girls here dying to dance with you. Go sweep one of them off their feet with those sexy eyes of yours."

He leaned down and winked at her. "No. See you tomorrow. I'm taking you to the beach for ice cream. I have a feeling you are going to need it."

Damn him.

She gave him a kiss on the cheek and walked back to Daniel, who was glaring at Cooper.

"Two seconds longer, Harper, and I wouldn't have been responsible for my actions," Daniel growled and wrapped his arm around her.

Harper sighed as they stepped into the lift. How had life gotten so complicated? Two amazing men, and she couldn't keep either of them.

Not really.

CHAPTER TWENTY-SIX

Daniel held the door open and followed Harper inside his penthouse suite. The cool air conditioning was a relief after hours in the tropical heat and all the alcohol he'd consumed.

"Drink?"

"Water, please," she answered, opening the sliding doors and stepping back out into the heat.

Daniel smiled and shook his head.

Harper had constantly been turning off any air conditioning while they were together. Coming from Manhattan, he'd still been adjusting to the temperature change, while she'd come from summer in New Zealand.

He'd never said anything to her.

Harper loved the heat. He had a feeling she'd hate New York in the winter. Handing her a chilled glass of water, he asked her.

"Do you like the snow?" She ran the glass over her collarbone, and it left a trail of moisture.

His cock hardened. "Harper. Fuck me."

She looked up, ignoring his reaction. "Does anyone love snow?"

Daniel glanced out across the beach. "Yes. Lots of people. For some, this would be the worst kind of vacation."

"They must be crazy."

"So do you? Like snow?"

"I don't know. I've never spent time in the white stuff. I've never seen it."

"You're joking, right?"

Harper shook her head.

"They have snow in New Zealand, I know they do. Great ski resorts," he said, frowning at her.

"Yes, loads of them. I just keep away from them. They're far too cold for me." Harper laughed. "In the winter, I head to one of the Pacific Islands for the warmth."

Daniel rested his hand on the lanai railing and smiled softly down at her. "You'd hate New York right now."

Harper moved into him, so he pulled her against his chest, his other hand landing on her hip. God, she felt simply perfect.

"I think a white Christmas would be romantic," she said, and Daniel rolled his eyes.

When she giggled, he was suddenly filled with ridiculous images of taking her skating in Central Park and doing all those cliché couple things. Daniel could just see her face light up at the sight of the enormous Christmas tree, and her nose rosy from the cold as they kissed while snow fell around them.

"If you lived there, you'd have to shovel snow and worry all the time about slipping. After the pretty stuff has fallen, it gets dirty," he said.

"When have you ever shoveled snow?" she asked, one brow raised.

Never.

"That's not the point. You'd hate it. No pretty sundresses or suntans," he said, running his finger over her bare shoulder.

She watched his eyes until they returned to hers.

"Then what *is* the point?" she asked. "Why am I here, Daniel?"

Good question.

Why?

Why, Daniel?

Because he couldn't stay away from her. Nothing was making sense anymore, and before he left, he had to have her one last time.

They both knew that's why she was here.

He ran his hand over her forehead, brushing her long dark locks off her face, then his lips lowered to hers gently.

He felt Harper's reluctance and stopped.

"I hate how I've hurt you. I hate not being with you," Daniel admitted. "I hate even more that I have to leave."

Harper's eyes dropped, then returned to his. "I feel the same, but we knew this was inevitable."

Was it?

Why was it?

God, nothing made sense. This woman, she'd turned everything he believed in, his well-structured life, into a kaleidoscope that didn't make sense anymore. He was questioning everything.

But he had things to say and needed to get them out.

"I know you believed I was lying to you. I wish you hadn't seen my father's text, so we'd had more time together," Daniel said. "I need you to know how much you mean to me, Harper. I've never spent time with another woman like we have. My bed, the sofa, the cars, they all feel empty without you."

He watched her slowly swallow and her eyes began to glisten.

"I watched you with that man and wanted to rip you out of his arms," Daniel growled, days of frustration rising up within him now.

Her mouth parted.

"Have you fucked him?" Harper tried to pull out of his arms, but he held her. "Answer me."

"No! God damn you, Daniel. How could you ask that?"

How could he not ask?

He gripped her arms tighter. "Because I want to scream and tell the world you're mine."

A tear escaped and slid down her distraught face.

"You can't do that. You can't do this to me," she cried. "You're leaving. I am leaving. That's the way it has to be."

She wasn't hearing him. He had to get her to understand. He needed her to know.

"Don't you hear what I'm saying?" She shook her head, refusing to look at him, but he continued. "I'm falling in love with you, Harper."

A guttural sound left her throat.

While tears poured down her face, Daniel slammed his mouth down on hers, taking complete possession.

One last time.

Harper responded, opening for him in surrender.

Daniel scooped her up and carried her to the bedroom, laying her down on the enormous bed. He kneeled over her as her hair fanned out over the luxury linens, making her look like a powerful Goddess.

She must be. She'd put a fucking spell on him.

"Oh, God," she moaned.

His eyes held hers before moving down her body, then he nudged the red straps off her shoulders and the flowing material quickly exposed her naked breasts. "This was a naughty dress to wear tonight. I wanted to strip you of it the moment I saw you."

She groaned.

He leaned down and plucked a pink nipple with his teeth, then sat down and tore his shirt off. Buttons went flying.

"Daniel." Harper half-laughed in surprise.

"It's just a shirt," he said, pulling her dress down. *Jesus.*

"What the hell?" His eyes snapped to hers. She returned his gaze, looking sultry and innocent all at once. "Where are your panties?"

Harper chewed her bottom lip. "They showed under the fabric so…"

He growled and gripped her thighs, pulling her down onto the bed. Removing his shorts, he grabbed a condom and threw it on the bed. One knee on the bed between her spread thighs, he gazed upon Harper's nakedness.

"Arms up," he said, taking her wrists above her head. Then he noticed she was wearing his watch. She saw the moment he noticed, and an overwhelming sense of possession powered through him. "Fuck."

He couldn't wait.

"Daniel," she begged, wanting the same thing.

"You're wet already, aren't you, baby?"

She nodded.

"Christ." His fingers slid through her and yes, she was soaked. His cock twitched with a raw need he'd never felt. "I need to be inside you. Right. Fucking. Now."

"Do it." She arched.

He maneuvered her and plunged inside in one movement. They both cried out together, Harper's arms ignoring his instruction and grabbing his biceps.

Thrust after thrust, he went deeper, taking as much of her as he could. Pleasure and dominance, unlike anything he'd experienced, overwhelmed him.

Harper writhed in ecstasy, her body moving in time with his, squeezing him, while little nails dug into his skin.

His arms slipped under her waist, half lifting her so their mouths were closer.

"Me, too." Harper gasped, and it took a second for him to register what she meant. "I'm falling in love with you, too."

His cock swelled and fire spiraled its way up his spine.

"Harper, shit," he cried and spilled into her. "Come, baby. Now. Come around my cock."

Her eyes widened, and she cried out as they came together.

A while later, he slid between her legs and tasted her. Sometime before morning, Harper woke him with her mouth on his cock and he'd thought he was in heaven.

Perhaps even better than heaven.

Daniel had then flipped her onto her knees while she gripped the ornate headboard and fucked her from behind. When his thumb ran over her ass, she'd cried out her fifth, or maybe sixth, orgasm.

Now they lay tangled in sheets, sweat glistening on their skin and more than totally sated.

At least their bodies were.

"I don't know what this means," she said against his chest while he ran his fingers over her hip.

He didn't either.

The feeling between them was so powerful. Surely, this sort of thing didn't come along very often. Neither of them could walk away from this.

Right?

She was his.

She felt like she belonged to him.

"Sleep, sweetheart. Let's talk in the morning." He kissed her gently and tucked her into his arms.

This beautiful mess was such a fuckup.

He was in no position to confess his love to someone right now with all the bullshit going on with the Mackenzie's.

But this was Harper, and he didn't think he could live without her.

CHAPTER TWENTY-SEVEN

"Thank you," Harper said as the server lifted the lid, exposing a full breakfast of eggs, bacon and all the trimmings.

They were dining outside in the sunshine on Daniel's lanai after a lazy, sexy morning. She felt blissfully exhausted.

When the serving staff left, Daniel leaned over and took her hand, pressing his lips to her knuckles. "You look thoroughly fucked, my love."

Harper let out a little laugh.

There was no humor in Daniel's eyes, however. They were dark and full of desire. Still. Even sitting here in a pair of shorts and a simple t-shirt, he exuded power. The fact both items of clothing cost more than her weekly income was beside the point.

Harper was aware they were back in their bubble, but she was glowing and wanted to stay there just for a little longer.

That he'd called her *his love* wasn't helping.

She wasn't completely naïve, though. At no point had Daniel said he wanted to be with her or asked if they could talk about being together. He had declared his love for her as if it was a life sentence and a source of pain, while being unable to walk away from her.

On some level, she understood. Harper was unable to get up and leave herself. So who was she to judge?

And yet, life was about to separate them. Daniel was flying home today, and she was departing a few days later.

Their bubble was about to burst.

"What time are you flying?" Harper asked, trying to be cool about it. "I guess you have your own private jet, right?"

Daniel nodded. "Yes, we have a fleet of Gulfstream Jets."

A fleet? Of course they did. She let out a snort.

"Does that bother you?" he asked.

She forked the egg into her mouth and shook her head. "No, I just don't know anyone with a private jet, let alone a fleet of them. Doesn't matter, I guess we truly are worlds apart. Sometimes I think I know you and then I realize I don't."

Daniel stared at her for a long moment.

"No, I guess you don't," he finally said. "I doubt you'd like me in my everyday life. I'm much less fun."

Harper swallowed and placed her utensils on her plate, frowning.

God damn him.

If he thought she was going to sit here while he spent the next hour telling her how much she would hate New York, hate him, hate his life, then he was wrong. It was like he was trying to find a way out of this.

He didn't need to.

If he didn't want her, then that was fine. Just fine. *Ugh.*

Why had she thought his declaration meant anything last night? Why had she let a slither of hope slip into her heart?

She was an idiot. Again.

"You don't need to do this," she mumbled, and he stopped, fork mid-way to his mouth.

"Do what?"

"Tell me all the reasons I won't like New York, or you, or the snow. I get it. You have a life, and I'm not going to be a part of it. I'm not asking for that, nor do I expect it, so please just stop." She said and then dropped her napkin on the plate, then stood. "You know what? I should just go."

Idiot, idiot, idiot.

Why had she let Daniel inside her heart again? God, she'd even told Daniel she loved him.

Idiot!

Through her anger, Harper couldn't help but think of the man downstairs who seemed more than willing to move mountains to be with her. *The world is a small place,* Cooper had said.

Harper shook her head.

This wasn't about Cooper.

It wasn't even about Daniel.

She had to believe that one day, somewhere, there was a man who would want her more than anything. Someone who would make her a priority and love her despite any obstacle.

She now realized that man was not Daniel Dufort.

"That's not…look, things are still complicated, Harper. I've never even dated a woman before, let alone told them I loved them," he said, dropping his utensils. "When I think of being with you, well, fuck, yes, I do worry you would hate New York. Not want me."

He stood and circled her as she searched for her phone and purse.

"Harper, stop. Come on. Don't go. I'm leaving in a few hours. Jesus, I told you I love you for God sakes. Give me time to wrap my head around all of this and sort some shit out."

She found her shoes and picked them up.

"Jesus, would you stop? I'll delay my flight another day. Then we can take some time and talk," he said, laying his hands on her shoulders from behind.

Harper turned.

"I know how this ends, Daniel. Tell me, would I be the most important thing in your life? Are you willing to get married?"

"Harper," he growled.

"Have you told your father you're not marrying that woman?"

Daniel paled and his jaw stiffened.

Unbelievable.

"Are you fucking kidding me?" she said, pushing him away as Daniel grabbed her wrists.

His phone began to ring.

"Crap. Fuck. What do you want, Fletcher?" Daniel snapped, punching the screen, clearly answering it instead of declining the call.

"So you've seen it?"

"Seen what?" he asked, a chill creeping through his bones.

Harper froze and looked up at him.

He knew what the next words were going to be as Fletcher began to speak. His mind was screaming, *fuck don't say it, don't fucking say it.*

But it was too late.

Even as he tried to turn the speaker off, the words were flowing.

"Daniel, the engagement announcement went out overnight. It's all over the news. Olivia has been trying to reach you."

As the blood left his face, he saw Harper's mouth fall open. "I'll call you back," Daniel said as Harper's eyes filled. One by one, tears fell down her face.

Daniel watched, feeling like his world was crumbling around him.

It was over.

He may be able to turn this bullshit around back home, but as his own heart cracked, he saw the same mirrored on the face of the woman in front of him.

The woman he loved.

Yet he had to try. "Please, Harper, I need to explain all of this."

She shook her head and a gut-wrenching noise escaped her. He pulled her into his arms, and she let him. "Fuck, Harper, I love you. If you believe nothing else, please know I fucking love you."

God damn it.

Harper was right—she deserved more than he could give her. In the end, it was unlikely he could give her what she wanted. He had so many other responsibilities which took priority, including his family, the business, and all this political bullshit.

Harper Kāne deserved a man who would put her on a pedestal like that lovesick puppy.

Daniel wasn't that man.

Harper pulled out of his embrace and wiped her eyes. "Well, congratulations, I guess," she said, letting out a God-awful laugh, and he wanted to throw up. "Goodbye, Daniel."

He stared at her. Just fucking stared at her as more tears fell, and then she turned and walked out.

Eventually, Daniel heard the door to the penthouse suite close. He followed the wake of her path until he reached the entrance.

On the table lay her Cartier watch.

CHAPTER TWENTY-EIGHT

Daniel reclined into the white leather seat of his private jet and tapped the tips of his fingers on the control panel. He was tempted to end the video call, turn on some mindless movie, and get trashed on whisky.

But that wouldn't solve a fucking thing.

Fletcher, Hunter, and Olivia were going back and forth, debating the media response to the Mackenzie press release about this bullshit engagement.

Daniel picked up his phone and his teeth ground together. Still no damn response from his father.

A crew member placed another coffee in front of him and he gave her a brisk nod, then reached for the cup of magic. He had no appetite and hadn't eaten a bite since, well, since breakfast with Harper.

Harper.

Daniel turned his head and stared out the window. Cloud after cloud rushed past.

He never expected to feel like this. Empty. Dazed. Like he didn't give a fuck.

Yet he did. He cared about his family business. He cared about his employees. He cared about his family. And he cared about Harper.

So how the hell was he going to fix this?

"Mr. Dufort, what would you like me to do? Every major network is asking for a response from you or the organization," Olivia said.

"Has anyone spoken to Dad?" he asked.

"No," Fletcher answered. "He's not answering any of our calls."

Shit.

"This is a fucking mess," Hunter said.

"I know I'm pressing, guys, but the longer we don't respond, the more speculation there will be," Olivia said. "We either confirm it or we don't, and we need to do it today."

Daniel snapped.

"No response," he growled and when everyone began to speak, he held up a hand, silencing them. "In case you've all forgotten, this is my personal reputation. We're debating, as well as Dufort Hotels, so the media can damn well wait until I have landed. If you need to say something, Olivia, tell them that."

Daniel ended the call and rubbed his forehead.

He felt ill.

The coffee was sitting in the pit of his stomach like concrete, and all he wanted to do was call Harper. But he knew she wouldn't answer.

Instead, he closed his eyes and tried to sleep.

An hour later, Fletcher's name flashed on the screen again.

"Fletch," he answered.

"Hunter and I are following a lead with the HR team. We'll meet at your apartment when you land and go over the details."

"Fine," Daniel replied.

"We're going to stop this," Hunter added.

"Do you have enough to undo this?" Daniel asked, and there was silence.

No, he didn't think so.

Less than two weeks ago, Daniel had accepted the possibility he may have to marry Nadia Mackenzie. He wasn't willing to go down without a fight, but now the stakes had changed.

Now he knew what love felt like and what he was losing. business

And it was more than just his single status.

Daniel knew now how it felt to stand beside a woman who held his heart and soul in the palm of her hand and want to protect her, care for her, and make love to her.

For better, for worse, for richer, for poorer, in sickness and in health, to love and to cherish, till death do us part. Those words had sounded like a death sentence to him for most of his life.

Now they were beginning to make sense.

"I need to get some sleep before we land," he said. "Let yourselves in, and I'll see you in a few hours. Don't drink all my fucking whisky."

Hunter smirked.

"Just get home," Fletch said, and the call ended.

God, he hoped they had something that would help.

Meanwhile, he really needed some sleep. He made his way down to the end of the plane to his bedroom and lay down.

He frowned as the feelings washed over him.

He'd love to have Harper on board the jet with him. She'd have so many damn questions and comments about how different their lives were.

She was right.

The way he lived was very different from most people, but it wasn't horrible. Couldn't Harper adjust? Hell, he'd spent years dodging women who wanted to be his wife because of his enormous wealth. Most people dreamed of the lifestyle he led.

Yet Harper seemed to have a strong dislike of it.

Didn't she know she'd never have to work another day in her life? Of course, Daniel knew she would—Harper had already achieved a level of success in her life, and he was really proud of her.

Sexy romance books might not be his cup of tea, but people wanted them just like they wanted a hotel room to sleep in. So who was he to judge?

Being together, though? It wasn't that easy for the two of them. Without a visa, Harper couldn't live in the United States. He would have to marry her.

Marriage.

That damn dirty word.

Daniel let out a long sigh. It was irrelevant—she would never forgive him. The most he could hope for was a professional relationship if they crossed paths.

It would be better if he accepted this right now and get focused on sorting out this extortion and his responsibility to Dufort Hotels, his staff, and his family.

Marriage wasn't for him.

Harper deserved someone who would put her first, and he wasn't able to do that.

Daniel flung his arm over his eyes and let out a sigh, then closed his eyes and attempted to sleep.

An hour before they landed, Daniel stepped into the shower for a quick rinse off. He leaned a hand against the wall and cursed a whole bunch.

Sleep hadn't helped.

He'd woken up looking for Harper after dreaming she had her hands on him. Tipping his head back, he let the water flow through his dark hair and added some shampoo. By the time he put the conditioner in, he was gritting his teeth.

Go down, for fuck's sakes.

Daniel reached for his cock and groaned. He knew well the feeling of her hand around him and the way her warm mouth felt as she took him deeply. Reluctantly, he stroked himself with a mix of regret and desire.

Would he never feel her in his arms again?

Would he never sink deep inside, feeling that rush of pleasure while their eyes held?

Her clit. Her swollen breasts.

Daniel squeezed his eyes and moaned as he released into his hand.

"Fuck, Dufort," he growled at himself. "You cannot lose this woman."

What was Harper doing right now? Did that lovesick asshole have his hands on her?

He brushed his teeth and spat into the marble sink and hissed. He leaned on the counter and took long, slow breaths.

Buzz, buzz.

Daniel pulled his phone out of his jeans pockets and saw Josh's number. Fuck, he hoped the guy had good news. He swiped to open the text.

Dufort, let's talk over a secure line when you are free.

I will be back in New York in a few hours.

Okay. I'll meet you by the Maine Monument in Central Park at 10:00 p.m. Alone.

As creepy as it sounded, Josh's message lifted Daniel's spirit. It was possible the black ops security team had some information which may assist in stopping Mackenzie. Then they'd only have a media fall out to clean up, but his team was totally capable of dealing with that.

In any case, it was the senator who had jumped the gun. An obvious attempt to put pressure on them, and one that would hopefully backfire on him.

Daniel had grand visions of sitting in front of the asshole, telling him he'd failed.

See you then.

He pocketed his phone and stepped out into the main cabin, throwing his winter coat and scarf over his arm. Gone were his shorts and t-shirts he wore in Hawaii with Harper.

He had some big fucking decisions to make.

One thing at a time.

First Mackenzie.

CHAPTER TWENTY-NINE

Daniel sat in the back of his Mercedes Maybach while his bags were loaded into the trunk. Moments later, they were speeding along the Lower Manhattan Expressway, heading home.

"Good trip, Mr. Dufort?" Jim, his driver, asked, glancing in the rearview mirror.

"Yes, thank you, Jim," he said, glancing back at the man who had worked for him for over five years. "It was nice to be away from the cold."

And to have a beautiful woman in my arms who meant something to me, but you know all about that because you are married. And I used to pity you. Now I'm wondering if I've been wrong.

"I'm not going to lie, sir. I'm envious. It's been damn cold."

Daniel looked up.

"Jim?" he said in question. "How did you know Kathy was the woman you wanted to spend the rest of your life with?"

Jim smiled, and it lit up his face.

"Oh, that's an easy one, sir. I simply couldn't breathe without her. She tried to leave me once because I was an idiot. It was hell. I couldn't see my life without her."

Daniel looked out the window, slowly nodding.

"You'll know," Jim said, surprising Daniel. He rarely spoke without prompt. "I might be out-of-place saying this, and perhaps you don't think I see or hear everything, but I do. You have a big heart, Mr. Dufort. People like us, we love big."

People like us?

"I just do what's right," Daniel replied, his eyes moving back inside the car. "But I don't think I have this time."

"If she's truly yours, you'll know."

Daniel turned back out the window and then, not knowing why, he murmured, "It's not Senator Mackenzie's daughter."

The press release was out, so people around America were already emailing and calling with congratulations. Each one making him feel more and more ill.

"Never thought it was, Mr. Dufort. Never thought it was."

The doorman dropped his bags inside the door and wished Daniel a good evening.

"Thank you," he said and stepped into his 57th Avenue apartment, on the infamous *Billionaire Row*. He pulled off his gloves and hung up his coat, just like it was any other winter night.

Except it wasn't. He didn't feel the same.

The expansive and architecturally designed apartment took over the entire top floor and had four bedrooms, three bathrooms, a private gym, an office, dining room, living room and chef's kitchen. Outside, a spacious balcony with two sets of luxury furniture overlooked Central Park.

He greeted his brothers, who were sitting in the living room while the enormous fireplace roared and threw out a warm glow against the soft neutral colors of the lounge suite. The painting above it looked as if it were moving as the shadows flickered against the canvas.

Daniel sat down, melting into the cushions.

"Drink?" Fletcher asked, walking over to the bar where a handful of crystal decanters sat filled with the best spirits one could buy. "By the way—"

Olivia wandered into the room, shaking her hands, indicating she'd just used his guest bathroom.

"Mr. Dufort," she said,

Fletcher lifted the glass, pointing at the woman. "Olivia is here."

"I see that. Hello, Olivia," Daniel replied, taking the crystal glass filled with dark golden liquid from his brother.

It was unusual, if not unheard of, for him to have an employee at his house. However, these were unusual circumstances, and he trusted Fletch had a good reason for bringing their PR Manager with them tonight.

"I hope you're not here to press for a media statement, because unless you are about to blow my God damn mind with some groundbreaking news, I'm not doing it," Daniel said.

Olivia sat beside Fletcher, and they shared a glance.

"What we're about to show you is a game changer. You're not going to like it," Fletcher said, pulling out a folder.

"Have you eaten?" Hunter asked, narrowing his eyes at him.

Daniel turned and stared out at the lights of Manhattan. He thought coming home would make him feel different, but it didn't. He simply felt far away from what was important.

His eyes drifted back to his brothers.

Get your ass back in the game, Dufort. These two matter. The business matters. Harper has moved on and will never forgive you this time.

He'd lost his chance. He should have stayed and fought for her. Instead, he let her walk away.

"Dan," Hunter repeated.

"Fuck," he cursed. "No, I haven't. Get whatever."

"We're going to fix this," Fletcher said, opening the file and taking a sheet from Oliva. He looked at Hunter. "Order a pizza."

"Pepperoni?" Hunter asked, swiping on his phone.

"Sure, whatever," Daniel said. "Now fucking show me what you have."

Fletcher moved the pile of books and candles from the coffee table and laid out some papers. Hunter finished the order and leaned in.

"Through some careful undercover investigation," Fletcher smirked at Olivia, who blushed. Daniel glanced between them. "We've learned that Suzanne Wrightson is dear old dad's longtime lover."

Christ.

"Or at least one of them," Hunter said, shaking his head.

"It appears he wasn't even loyal to his fucking lovers," Fletcher added.

Daniel leaned back on the couch, lifted his ankle onto his knee and draped an arm across the cushions. "So? This is hardly breaking news."

Olivia wriggled forward and picked up a document. "Except we believe this is different. He paid her a bunch of cash and set her up in a nice house in Brooklyn about ten years ago."

He took the paper from her and scanned it. "Who owns it? Or more to the point, whose name is it in?"

"She does. The title is in Suzanne's name."

Daniel glanced up from the paper, looking between his brothers and Olivia. "Okay, what am I missing here? Dad's not the first wealthy man to set up an old lover with a home."

As sickening as it was, that was a fact. He wouldn't be surprised if Johnathan had purchased a number of homes and gifted them on to get out of a pickle or two before he'd divorced their mother.

"A former co-worker of Suzanne's knew about the situation, and the two women have kept in touch. A few months ago, Suzanne found out about the other lovers. She believed she was the only *other* woman in Johnathan Dufort's life," Olivia said.

"Really? That seems…naïve," Daniel said, but then shook his head. "And she's pissed?"

Olivia and Fletcher both nodded.

"Highly," Hunter added.

"A woman scorned, and all that," Olivia said, shrugging.

"You know who she is, right? Suzanne from legal. She works with Brent and has access to the locked vault with the legal documents."

Well, shit. Daniel stared at the papers in front of him.

"Do we have proof?"

"We have video footage of her going into the vault," Fletcher said, lifting his phone. "However, for her job, Suzanne needs to access it from time to time. Unfortunately, we don't have the technology to zoom in and prove it was the document she took."

No, but Daniel knew someone who did, and he was meeting with him tonight.

"Send me the file," he instructed. "If we can get the proof, how do we link her to Mackenzie? I'm assuming that's where you're going with this."

Hunter nodded and tossed back the whisky in the bottom of his tumbler. "Yup."

"We haven't yet, but we will," Fletch said, gathering up the documents now spread across his coffee table.

Daniel stood and walked to the floor-to-ceiling glass windows and swirled the whisky around and around.

There would be a link.

They'd done a good job uncovering this information, but it was time to bring in the big guns. In another hour he'd be meeting with Josh, and regardless of what news he gave him, he was going to get *Black Hawke Security* to close the loop on this.

"Get HR to prepare Suzanne's dismissal papers, but hold them for twenty-four hours," he said with his back to the room.

She had to be removed from the business, but not until he had all the information they needed. Suzanne may be a victim in all of this, but she'd broken the law and put billions of dollars, and people's livelihoods, at risk here. Not to mention his fucking life.

As for his father…

"What does Johnathan know?" Daniel asked.

"Nothing. Yet," Fletcher replied.

Daniel turned and pushed one of his hands in his pockets, his eyes on the people in his living room. What Daniel was about to do was step into an incredibly gray area of the law. Also known as *outside of it.* He was a wealthy and powerful man. If anyone caught even a whisper of what he was about to do, it could destroy him and the Dufort Dynasty.

The less people that knew about this, the better. More importantly, he needed to know exactly who knew what.

"Olivia," he said, capturing her attention. "Send me a list of all the people in your team who are privy to this investigation."

He watched as she immediately turned to Fletcher for a response. Fletch might be her manager, but Daniel was unimpressed.

"Oliva," he demanded, and her head whipped back to him with wide eyes. His own narrowed. "Do I need to remind you who the chief executive of Dufort Hotels is?"

"No, sir," she said quickly.

"Daniel," Fletcher warned, and Daniel shot him a look, silencing him. He rarely got authoritative with his brothers, and never in front of their teams, but he was unimpressed with Fletcher's response. Right now they weren't brothers, they were colleagues.

"Tell me who else knows," he said, his eyes scanning back to Olivia.

She chewed her lip, thinking.

"No one. Wait, one of my team knows I've been working on a special project, but they don't know any details," she said, then added, "All my meetings have been in Fletch's—sorry, Mr. Dufort's—office, so it's been properly contained."

Fletch? Daniel raised a quick brow at his brother, who glanced away.

"Keep it that way," Daniel said, dropping his glass on a table. "From now on, everything we discuss is highly classified. I mean that for your own safety."

Fletcher frowned angrily. "That's unnec—"

Daniel's patience snapped.

"Oh, come on, Fletcher, we're talking about a fucking US senator. You don't think he'll play even dirtier when we uncover whatever the fuck this is?"

Fletcher shook his head.

"You think Dad is tied up in something?" Hunter asked.

"Maybe. Maybe not," Daniel said. "But, and Olivia, fucking classified all right. If he's a liability to the security of this company, then it could be time he stood down."

"Fuck," Hunter cursed.

"Jesus, Daniel," Fletcher said, standing up and pacing.

Yeah, that.

He realized what he was saying was huge, but they all knew his father wouldn't stand down. He'd built the Dufort Dynasty with his bare hands and Daniel respected the hell out of him for it, but he would not stand by and let him destroy it.

Or his damn life.

His father had been willing to marry him off because he'd fucked up by not keeping his cock in his pants. Just like he'd fucked up his marriage and nearly destroyed their mother. Daniel was done. He'd show his father just how fucking powerful his son, the CEO, was.

"It's my job to protect Dufort Hotels, and that's what I'm doing. He'd do the same if he were in my shoes again. Or at least he fucking should," Daniel said, shaking his head.

Hunter sat shaking his head, but he could tell his little brother knew he was right. He was pragmatic but also incredibly loyal. They all were—none of this was going to sit right with any of them.

Fletch sat back down and flung his arm on the back of the sofa behind Olivia. Her eyes darted to him briefly and then lowered.

What the hell?

Fletcher glanced down at Olivia, then back to Daniel. "Do we need to talk this out? I can see Olivia out."

The doorbell rang, and Hunter went to collect the pizza.

"No. Until I have more information, there's not a lot more to add to that. Olivia, where are we with the media?" Daniel asked, sitting down once more.

She took a slice of pizza and licked her thumb. "Well, if you confirm the engagement, then you'll always have a broken engagement on your record. They'll bring it up forever," she said, taking a bite and chewing it hungrily.

Hell, had any of them eaten?

God, he was so consumed with this mess he'd kept them working all damn evening. Still, they were grown ass adults.

"I *could* talk to my contacts and tell them the other camp had jumped the gun. Then promise exclusivity once you're ready. Which we won't, of course, but it will buy us time."

"Will it work?"

"Yes, but only for a short time. Like a day. You need to know it will damage our relationships with them," Olivia added.

"Which is not ideal, but we need to weigh up the risks here," Fletcher said. Ultimately, the decision was Daniel's, but Fletcher was the head of marking for Dufort Hotels, so he also had a play in the decision.

Not to mention his brothers were shareholders.

"Board members have been emailing," Hunter added

Daniel pressed his lips together. "Yeah, I've had a couple of emails. I'm not responding, obviously." Daniel swirled his whisky again, thinking. "The broken engagement. Do we care? From a brand reputation perspective?"

"The company doesn't. Frankly, it's just gossip," Fletcher answered. "Your love life is constantly in the news, so it's a big deal, but it's not going to bump share prices either way."

"It's not just his love life in the news, Romeo," Hunter laughed.

Daniel actually felt his face crack when he smirked. That's how long it had been since he'd smiled.

When he didn't hear Fletch give their brother shit back, he frowned. He looked up and instead he was giving Hunter the bird while munching on his pizza, but there was something up with him.

Olivia cleared her throat uncomfortably. "What I would consider, Mr. Dufort, is the day you actually get engaged. You and the future Mrs. Dufort—your fiancée—will have to deal with the previous broken engagement, though fake, being mentioned over and over."

Hunter snorted. "Dan's never getting married. None of us are."

Olivia shot him a questioning look, then glanced at Fletcher, who shrugged.

What the hell was up between those two? Daniel watched them for a moment but was distracted by the image in his mind, which wouldn't disappear.

Harper with a ring on her finger, dealing with the New York media on what should be the happiest days of her life. Even though he'd lost her, Daniel found he still held the tiniest string of hope, which helped form his decision.

"Stall them," he instructed.

"Yes, sir," she said, nodding and stood.

"I'll see you home," Fletcher said, stuffing his phone and wallet in his pockets. "Later."

He watched Olivia pack up her things and throw her bag over her arm. She politely said goodbye and then glanced at Fletcher, who placed his hand *nearly* on the small of her back. He stopped himself and then walked her out of the room.

When he heard the door close, Daniel stretched out his legs and stared at his little brother. "Want to tell me what the fuck is going on between those two?"

"Nope," Hunter said, all *leave me out of it.*

Daniel shook his head. "Fuck me, I don't have time for this right now."

It went against Dufort company policy for any of the executive team to be romantically (read: have sex with) involved with staff.

Daniel had created the new policy when he became CEO two years earlier. The HR team had spent decades cleaning up after their father's, and other leaders, unethical behavior. With new employment laws, it was the right thing to do. Daniel would speak to Fletcher once this Mackenzie debacle was all over.

He fucking hoped it would be over.

Right now, Daniel needed to get down to Central Park to meet Josh Hawke.

"Go home. Get some sleep," he told Hunter. "I suspect tomorrow is going to be a huge day."

CHAPTER THIRTY

"Harper, open up. I know you're in there!" the voice added to the incessant knocking.

How? How did he find out which room she was in?

"Harper Kāne, I swear I will bribe the housekeeper to unlock this door as well if you don't open it!" Cooper yelled.

So that's how he knew. Harper frowned and pulled the door open. "You bribed the housekeeper?" she growled, one hand on her hip.

"You're in the penthouse?" Cooper asked, raising a brow.

She shrugged and walked inside, knowing he'd follow. "You know, I could get her fired for telling you where I was staying."

When he didn't respond, she turned around.

"No, you won't, because I'm not telling you which one it was. And don't be sexist, it could have been a guy."

Despite herself, Harper smiled.

"See, you're happier now that I'm here." Cooper grinned, stepping closer.

Harper shook her head. Right now, all she could feel was the pain in her heart. Daniel was likely back in New York by now, and the distance between them felt as big as a black hole.

Harper had cried for hours when she'd returned to her room this morning. Screaming into her pillow, then standing in the shower, berating herself for getting involved with yet another man that was wrong for her.

"I can't do this right now, Coop," Harper said, and walked outside, plonking down on the wicker sofa.

Cooper sat opposite her in a matching chair.

"I know what happened," he said, and she glanced up. "I saw the news. Fucking prick."

Heat flashed across her face. Harper was ashamed, along with all the other emotions she was dealing with. She hated that her three amigos thought she knew about this other woman when she hadn't.

"Daniel told me he was single. He assured me," she spat out.

"I'm not judging you."

"Yes, you are. Along with everyone in this hotel who saw me with Daniel."

Cooper got up and sat beside her. He looked down at her with such intensity she nearly had to look away. "No, they won't. You're too lovable," he said. "Men like Daniel Dufort have a reputation, so no one is going to judge you. They'll judge him."

Harper knew he was trying to make her feel better, but something about the way he referred to Daniel in that way didn't sit right.

She could clear his name right now by telling Cooper about Daniel's father pressuring him into the marriage, but that wasn't hers to share.

Perhaps she was a fool, or perhaps she was just in love, but on some level, she didn't believe Daniel had really set out to be deceitful. Perhaps he truly thought the marriage wouldn't need to go ahead?

He had looked as shocked and angry as she had felt.

"You can just tell me I was an idiot. You don't need to be nice." She frowned.

Cooper shook his head.

"That's your problem, Harper. You don't believe you deserve nice. Once you do, the right man will show up. Anyway, I'm not nice. Trust me."

She looked up at him and blinked.

Did he really believe that? Cooper was amazing. If she hadn't met Daniel, Harper knew she would be absolutely charmed by him.

"Yes, you are, Coop. You're perfect. I should want you. Or, you know, someone like you."

He stared at her for a long moment, and she saw the fire brewing in his eyes.

Oh boy, what have I done?

"You don't know me, Harp," he said. "I know you're broken-hearted right now, but we only have a few days left together. Spend the day with me. The guys are nursing hangovers on the beach, so let's hang out. Just us."

Harper glanced away.

"I don't know, Cooper."

Just the thought of it felt like she was betraying Daniel.

He'd be furious if he saw Cooper sitting her with her, his arm along the back of the sofa around her. Yet Daniel was on the other side of the planet, preparing to marry a senator's daughter.

He hadn't texted her.

He hadn't tried to stop her from leaving.

He had done nothing.

Daniel had left and returned to his life in New York, forgetting her.

"Plus," he said, turning her chin and winking at her. "I've got money. Maybe not as much as Dufort, but I could splash out on a penthouse or two."

Harper frowned at him and batted his hand away. "Stop it, you know I'm not like that. If anything, his money was scary."

"Scary?" Cooper laughed.

Harper shrugged. It was hard to explain to people who had money, and she'd figured out pretty early on Cooper had a bit more than he was making out.

"Intimidating," she answered. "How could I ever fit into a billionaire lifestyle?"

Cooper leaned back into the cushions of the sofa and shook his head. "That guy is an asshole. You should never have felt that way, Harper. I might not be a billionaire—*yet*—but let me show you how to be with a rich man and enjoy it."

Yet?

Harper was suddenly filled with a dozen questions. She narrowed her eyes at him. "How rich exactly are you, Cooper?"

He leaned in and smiled. "See, that's the difference between him and I—I'll never tell. Old money, sweetheart. Old money."

Harper didn't know what that meant, but she couldn't help but laugh at him. Daniel had never talked about his wealth, but Cooper didn't know that.

His charm was putting a smile on her face, so she let out a sigh and decided at the very least she needed to get out of the hotel.

"No promises, Coop," she said.

He stood and held out his hand, ever the gentleman. She took it and lifted her to her feet. "I'll be back in thirty minutes to collect you," he drawled and lifted her fingers to his lips. "Dress pretty."

Then left.

Harper sighed. She had just over two days left on the island. Nothing was going to change what had happened between her and Daniel.

He was gone.

She hadn't come to Hawaii looking to meet a man, and yet she had. Two of them. Both gorgeous and wealthy. It was like something from one of her novels.

One of them she had fallen in love with, and he'd broken her heart. The other was just a friend, but she wondered if her Daniel blinkers had blocked her from seeing any other possibility with Cooper.

Did she owe it to them both to at least consider it?

She could draw a line in the sand and tell Cooper she wanted to just be friends, or she could give him—give them both—this opportunity to see if there was something more there.

What did she have to lose?

She'd lost Daniel already and couldn't deny Cooper made her feel like she was number one. Heck, she'd been looking for that her entire life.

Harper stood in the shower and ran her hands over her body. The memory of Daniel's touch was still raw. She couldn't imagine anyone making her body burn like Daniel Dufort and the fact he was now a story from her past made tears fall down her face again.

How on earth was she going to get over him?

Harper dressed in a midi-length white sundress for their date. She had no idea where they were going, so she added her small white crossbody handbag, and last minute plonked her beige sunhat on her head.

The closer it got to Cooper picking her up, the more unsure Harper felt about this, but she'd agreed to go, and she'd just be honest with him about how she was feeling.

Plus, she couldn't deny there *was* a little something between them. She hadn't lied when she said if she'd met him before Daniel, she would have been completely charmed by Cooper.

But she hadn't.

Turning her love for Daniel off wasn't going to happen overnight.

Change of plans. Meet me downstairs. Cooper text.

Harper grabbed her room card and left.

When the lift pinged open, she stepped out into the large foyer and glanced around. The reception was busy with people checking in, and the sad-looking people standing outside with their suitcases were those leaving the island.

Soon it would be her.

She slowly made her across the lobby and took a seat.

"Harper!" Cooper called, walking through the front doors.

"Oh, hey," she said, jumping up. "I'm sorry. Were we meeting out there?"

He shook his head and grinned.

Suddenly, Harper noticed he looked different. Gone were his casual t-shirts, replaced by a light blue short-sleeved shirt, and long white resort style shorts. He looked fresh, tanned and, well, very good looking.

"Wow," he said. "You really know how to follow instruction." She frowned in confusion, and he laughed. "You look pretty, Harper. Come on, let's go."

She blushed at his compliment and was starkly aware of Daniel's staff seeing her with another man. Then she mentally kicked herself for being an idiot.

He no longer cared. She had to get on with her life.

Cooper led her outside to a black *Audi A5* convertible. He opened the door, and she climbed in, giving him a questioning look. He winked and moved to the driver's seat.

"Are you trying to impress me?" she asked, smiling.

"Absolutely," Cooper replied as he slid on his sunglasses, started the car, and drove them out of the hotel driveway. "Is it working?"

It was a bit.

"Maybe," was all she said, and they both grinned as he drove them out of Waikiki.

Twenty minutes later, she asked where they were going. She knew Oahu enough to know they were heading east, which was an affluent part of the island.

"We can go anywhere we want, but I'm taking you for a picnic at a favorite beach of mine."

"Wait. Favorite? How many times have you been here?"

He shrugged. "Like, a lot. My family has a house here."

She turned to him in surprise. "Then why are you staying at the hotel?"

He shrugged. "The boys wanted to. It's a boys' trip. No big deal. Anyway, it's handy being right in Waikiki."

Harper shook her head. He was full of surprises. As they continued along the beautiful coastline, she took a few photos, then focused back on her driver.

"Were they upset to be left behind? Grayson and Luke?"

"Yes, but they said they'd forgive me if I married you."

Shocked, Harper let out a big laugh. "Good luck with that. I'm never getting married."

Cooper glanced at her, then back at the road as they pulled into a large parking lot of a beach park. "Ever?"

She shrugged. "Probably not."

He sighed. "Come on."

Harper just shrugged again and got out of the car. "Wow, this place is beautiful."

It felt relaxed, peaceful, and more private than the popular tourist beach in Waikiki. They found a spot to sit, and Cooper laid out a blanket and placed a large picnic basket beside them. She teased him about being a romantic as he pulled out a bottle of champagne, glasses, tropical fruits, cheeses, and meats.

"Hey, I spent all day putting this together," he said.

"Liar," she laughed. "Did the hotel do it?"

"A gentleman never tells," Cooper said, handing her a glass with golden bubbles.

"A toast," she said, crossing her legs and facing him. "To holidays in Hawaii, wonderful new friendships…and suntans."

Cooper cringed. "Wow, you must be a terrible author."

"What? Why?" she asked, surprised but laughing.

"That's a really terrible toast. Let me try," he said as she lifted her glass once more, giving him a look. "To serendipitous meetings, slow dances at sunset and open hearts."

Harper held his eyes, reflecting on the past few days she'd spent with Cooper. She was right, he was a romantic.

"You win," she said quietly, and they both took a sip. Harper looked away, not ready to go deeper with him just yet.

They nibbled at the food and chatted about their families and what it was like growing up. Cooper was from New Orleans. He'd spent years living in Massachusetts while at Harvard, going home for vacations or meeting them in Hawaii.

He had a PhD in neuroscience and explained he'd spent nearly nine years studying.

"So, what are you going to do now?"

"Honestly, I'm not sure," Cooper said. "This holiday has been about letting loose and then I am heading home to New Orleans and will sit down with my parents and discuss it."

Harper shook her head.

"I just can't imagine talking to anyone else about my life plans. I'm so independent," she said.

The last thing Harper would do was take advice from her mother. She loved her, but she'd always worked a minimum-wage job and was pretty miserable about life. So she was hardly the world's best life coach.

Cooper shrugged. "Luke was being an ass the other day, but he's right. Both Graydon and I are trust-fund babies. With that comes benefits and expectations. It's drummed into us all our lives. I've been away from home a long time, and now I need to decide what I want."

"And find a job."

He laughed. "Yes. Maybe."

Maybe?

"Surely you won't waste your PhD and nearly a decade of education."

"No. It won't ever be a waste. But do I want to be a neuroscientist? I'm not sure," Cooper said.

"Right, but you have money, so you don't need to race out and get a job."

"I get it. It makes me sound like an asshole," he said.

"No. It's just a different way of living, I guess," Harper said. "I don't have that luxury. If I don't work, my bills don't get paid."

"Do you want to stay in New Zealand?" he asked, resting on his elbow with his long legs stretched out.

Harper still had her legs crossed and was chewing on the last of the strawberries.

Did she want to stay in New Zealand?

She wasn't sure.

With dual citizenship, because her father was Hawaiian, moving to the United States had been on her mind recently. Not because of Daniel. Not because of the contract with *BookFlix*. She'd just felt a pull to do it since David had left her. It would mean leaving Kristen and many of her other friends, but there was a knowing something more was out there for her.

"No," she answered honestly.

It was late in the afternoon, and the sun behind them was beginning to drop.

"We won't see a sunset here," Cooper said, glancing behind him when he saw her glance at the sky. "But I thought you'd like it here. It's quiet."

"It's perfect," she said, shifting to settle on one hip.

"Here." Cooper placed some towels behind them, as pillows, and leaned against them, his arms behind his head. "Lie down."

She looked at him hesitantly.

"I don't bite, Harper," he said gently. "In fact, you're going to have to make the first move. *If* you want to."

Harper wasn't sure how to respond, but she knew she could trust him. If there was one word to describe how she felt about Cooper from the moment they'd met, it was comfortable.

She lay beside him, looking at the darkening sky, using his bicep as a pillow.

"The sky looks different in New Zealand," she said. "Would you ever come to visit me?"

"Without hesitation," he answered

Harper smiled.

That was what she wanted. Someone who put her first and moved heaven and earth to be with her. Someone who made her a priority and damn everything else. Yet it seemed so hard to believe anyone would, or could, ever want her that much.

"Really?" she asked, turning to him. "Just that easy?"

"It's not easy, Harper, but yes, I would," Cooper said, tilting his head to look down at her. "Why the hell wouldn't I?"

Her brain misfired as images of Daniel and Cooper merged. Feelings and emotions from nearly two weeks of these two men competed for space in her brain. Could it be she wanted the wrong man?

Had Daniel simply been a path to Cooper?

Was he the man she was supposed to love?

She could barely think with Cooper's green eyes on hers, and his large body up against hers, just as a lover would. His hard bicep under her head wasn't helping anything, either.

No man had ever gone out of his way to put together a romantic picnic for her before. Or hired a fancy car to impress her. Cooper had dropped his friends and put her first. He wasn't just a man of words; he was following up with actions.

She was important to him.

Joy in the moment fought with sadness that she hadn't even been worth a goodbye text from Daniel.

So, it was time to move on.

Cooper stared at her, the intensity building in his eyes. Harper recognized his desire, his need, and the warmth that radiated off him. She had a sudden desire to place her hand on his chest and be closer to him.

"If you keep looking at me like that, you are going to make a liar out of me, Ms. Kāne," he said, a small smirk on his lips.

Nice lips.

Different lips to those last night.

Kind lips.

Truthful lips.

Suddenly Harper realized, yet again, she had not asked any questions. She sat up and *did* place a hand on his chest this time.

Cooper lifted his head. "What's wrong?"

"Are you single?"

He flopped down and groaned.

"Well, are you?"

Cooper looked back at her. "Yes, Harper, I am single. No secret fiancée, girlfriends, lovers or wives anywhere."

"Boyfriend?" she asked, then shrugged at his reaction. "What? I'm just covering all the bases."

Next minute she was flat on her back with a larger than she'd realized Cooper over her.

"No one else. Full stop," he said while her heart pounded. "Now, are you going to kiss me, Harper Kāne, or are you going to make me break my promise?"

She nodded.

She had to do this. She wanted to do this. She wanted to kiss Cooper.

She liked him, and she needed to know if there were sparks. Maybe not like with Daniel, but he wasn't hers anymore, and she was here with this amazing man.

Harper moved toward his mouth, but that was all she had to do. Cooper needed no more encouragement. His arms swooped under her and pulled her against his body, his mouth taking ownership of hers.

She flung her arms around his neck and opened to him. Warmth flowed through her as their bodies connected. His kiss was wanting, knowing, and demanding. After a time, Cooper's lips moved across her cheek, to her jaw and down her neck.

"Fuck, I knew kissing you would be amazing," Cooper said.

And it was a wonderful kiss. He felt like all the delicious characters she wrote about. Strong and perfect, charming, and protective. Sex with Cooper would be incredible, she had no doubt.

His mouth took hers again, and she melted into it, feeling the heat between them build. He groaned, then lifted his head and gazed down at her.

"Now I regret driving so far away from the hotel," he said, and she smiled.

Harper's eyes drifted, and he cupped her face. "You're not okay with this, are you?"

"It's been less than a day, Coop."

He groaned.

"God, I'm sorry. But fuck, tell me you felt that kiss, Harper. Please tell me I wasn't alone."

"You weren't," she said, pressing into him closer. "Cooper, you weren't. There is something between us but..."

"But I'm not him?"

"No, it's just…"

"You love him," Cooper said.

She nodded. "Yes."

Cooper sat up and leaned on his knees. He shook his head a few times. "One damn week. If we'd arrived one week earlier, I would have met you before him."

She smiled and hooked her arm under his, snuggling into him. Cooper wrapped his arm around her, and they sat there looking across the now dark water.

"Just give me time. My heart's broken and yet I have feelings for you. It's confusing," Harper said. "I feel guilty being here with you and yet for all I know, he's in Manhattan right now putting a ring on it, you know?"

Cooper tipped her head. "You have nothing to feel guilty about. He left you. He lied to you. And we have every right to explore this."

She knew everything he said was true, yet her heart ached deeply to feel Daniel's arms wrapped around her.

But he was gone.

CHAPTER THIRTY-ONE

Daniel dug his hands into his coat pocket and walked toward the Maine Monument. He wasn't surprised he couldn't see Josh yet—it was why he got paid the big bucks.

And when he said big bucks, he meant BIG bucks.

Which was hopefully about to pay off.

A couple took a selfie, then shared a kiss. Daniel briefly closed his eyes. Every bone in his body was screaming at him to text or call Harper and tell her he loved her and was flying across the fucking planet to abduct her, whether or not she liked it.

And offer her what? Life as his lover and illegal alien in the United States?

Nice one, Daniel.

With his connections, he could probably arrange a visa for her, but Harper deserved more than that. She deserved the romantic proposal in Central Park, or on a tropical beach, with the man she loved down on one knee. She deserved the five-carat emerald-cut diamond ring from Tiffany's and a lavish engagement party with people celebrating their love.

Our love.

She deserved the wedding dress of her dreams and to be a princess for the day as she walked down the aisle to the man who couldn't live without her, gazing at her with wet eyes. All that stuff women wanted.

But afterward came life. Reality. And usually ended in divorce and heartbreak. He couldn't do that to Harper, even if he could get himself out of this current fucking mess.

And he had no idea how long it would take.

Was he even capable of being a husband? A good husband?

The real question was, could he live without her? She belonged with him; he was sure of it. He could feel it in his heart.

"Dufort," a dark voice said as it stepped out of the shadows.

He greeted Josh, and they walked along the path into Central Park where they could talk.

"Do I need to frisk you?" he asked.

Daniel let out a dry laugh. "No, but you are most welcome to."

The man studied him, then continued.

"We have everything you need to get this fucker off your back," he said, getting straight to the point, and a shiver ran through Daniel's body. "And more."

Daniel slowed, but Josh shook his head. "Keep walking. This is too sensitive to risk being overheard."

Jesus.

"How do we do this?"

He felt the man's hand slip into his pocket and drop something. "Listen to this tonight, then put it somewhere with your most valuable possessions. We have cut the classified government information for your protection. What you need has been left, but Dufort, it's still fucking dangerous."

"Got it. Thank you."

Daniel wasn't shocked. He'd known what it meant to tap a US senator, and he wasn't proud of it.

Mackenzie had started this mess. What did he think was going to happen? That Daniel was going to polish his wedding shoes and smile as the man's God damn daughter walked down the aisle toward him?

"Let me know if you'd like our services once you listen to it. If not, I'll send you an invoice and we are done."

Daniel walked as he thought.

"Is he going to be taken care of anyway?" he asked, referencing the comment Josh had made during their last conversation.

"You don't want me to answer that," he said. "It wouldn't be within the timeframe you need, anyway."

Daniel narrowed his eyes, then slowed and turned. "Timeframe?"

"Ms. Kāne isn't going to wait forever," he said, shrugging.

"How the fuck do you know about Harper?" he growled, forgetting for a moment who he was talking to.

"It's my job to know everything, Dufort."

"You had me followed?" Daniel growled. "That wasn't part of the fucking deal, Josh."

"All my clients are monitored while we work together. Call it a trust issue." Josh shrugged. "Check the fine print under distance monitoring. Or some fucking clause."

They both knew there was no contract or clause.

"I guess I should've expected it," Daniel said, running his hand over his hair. "Creepy as fuck, though."

He knew that was the deal when you dealt with men like this. They had their own rules.

Josh laughed.

As they walked farther, the big man clamped him on the shoulder. "I like you, Dufort. If you want my advice, I'd get your ass back to Hawaii before the choice is taken from you. Fuck all this," he said, waving his arm around at the city. "Power, money, control."

Would he give it all up for Harper?

Maybe.

Daniel had a responsibility to his family and his employees, but he also had to consider what was best for Harper.

Could he be the man she wanted? Daniel didn't do things half-heartedly in life, but he had no idea how to be a husband or even a fucking boyfriend. When he looked at the man who taught him everything he knew, he cringed. Johnathan Dufort had been a terrible husband. His mother had suffered terribly, and there was no way he wanted to do that to Harper.

Hell, look at how miserable he'd already made her!

The next morning, he called Fletcher and Hunter over for an early breakfast after listening to the recording approximately ten million times.

They were drinking the last of their coffee when he decided to hit Fletcher up. "Did Olivia get home okay?"

Fletcher avoided his eyes and nodded. "Yeah. I put her in an Uber."

"Were you in it with her?" Daniel asked.

Fletcher's head snapped up. "Yes. Then I left her at the doorstep. Jesus."

Daniel's eyes held his.

"You know the rules, Fletcher. Find someone else to play with."

God knows his brother had his pick of the bunch. With those bright blue eyes and square fucking jaw, his brother was a damn liability. He'd always chosen the wrong girl in society. The one who was promised to another man, or some damn untouchable princess.

The only consolation—and these were Fletcher's words—was that he was so good in bed the women kept their lips closed.

Not their legs, apparently, but their lips.

"I'm not *playing* with Olivia," Fletch snapped. "She's a valuable member of the team and we have been working closely together to help *you.*"

"She likes you."

Fletcher shrugged, grinning. "I'm likeable."

Daniel rolled his eyes.

"Dear God. His ego knows no bounds." Hunter said.

"Oh, excuse me, Shakespeare."

"That's not Shakespeare, idiot."

Daniel usually enjoyed their brotherly banter, and, for a moment, he was pleased to be home, but he had to stay focused and get back to his original reason for calling them here. But he wasn't done.

"I'm serious, Fletch. You can't go there. We're clear on that, aren't we?"

Fletcher placed his coffee loudly on the table. "Drop it, Daniel," Fletcher growled. "I know the fucking rules. Now what the fuck are we doing here? Because unless you've forgotten, my team has a media crisis on our hands."

Interesting.

He did drop it. For now. But he was keeping an eye on that space.

"Get comfortable," he said, and pressed play on his laptop. After they had listened to it and their mouths dropped, he slammed the laptop closed.

"Mother fucker," Hunter exclaimed.

"That prick is going down," Fletcher said, standing and pacing. "Asshole."

He gave them a moment longer to let it sink in, allowing the now familiar flush of fury to wash over him. No matter how many times he listened, Daniel wanted to force his way into the senator's office and punch the old guy.

That wasn't an option. And it wouldn't solve anything. He needed a clear head and a plan.

"How did you get this?" Hunter asked, pointing to the laptop.

Daniel shook his head. "Don't ever ask me that again."

Both his brothers stared at him, then nodded.

"You need to stop protecting us," Fletcher said. "We're not kids anymore, Daniel."

He didn't care how old they were. It was his duty to protect them, and everyone in his company.

"I will always protect you, so fuck off. It's my job as your big brother and duty as the CEO of Dufort Hotels."

"You really think that?"

"Yes," he growled, then got them back on track. "Now we need to decide what to do about this. None of it can be used as evidence, so taking legal action is not an option here."

During the conversation, the US senator had shared that he'd been planning his run for president for a long time and had planted seeds to fund it over the years.

Johnathan Dufort had never been a target until the night he'd found him with his hands on his wife. The two were old college buddies and were well known scoundrels, but it was an unwritten rule that you didn't touch another man's wife.

That was when he decided to change the rules of their agreement. He knew he wouldn't take long for Johnathan to dig himself a hole and when his friend had told him about the situation with Suzanne, Mackenzie had laid the foundation for what was now playing out.

Mackenzie knew Suzanne and stayed in casual contact with her over the years, helping her out if she needed it. Then, boom, just in time for the agreement to be paid out, Mackenzie tells her she wasn't Johnathan's only lover during that time of their lives.

All those promises that she was the love of his life, but he couldn't be with her because of his wife and kids, suddenly meant nothing. His explanation that because of the Dufort Dynasty, they couldn't be together was an obvious lie.

Suzanne was furious, of course. Makenzie then offers her the opportunity to get revenge and sweetens the deal by offering her two million dollars. All she has to do is retrieve the document from the Dufort vault.

As Olivia said, *a woman scorned.*

It was a fucking lot of money for the average person to say no to, let alone a woman betrayed.

And Mackenzie knew it.

Daniel ran his hand over his face.

The way Daniel saw it they had two options available to them: they could confront Mackenzie and share a snippet of the recording, or he could hire *Black Hawke* and let them deliver a nice juicy threat on behalf of the Dufort's.

Effective but dirty.

The Dufort Dynasty wasn't dirty, and it wasn't in Daniel's playbook—unless he was pushed.

He was a powerful player in New York City and no wallflower to sit across from in the boardroom. Now that he had cards to play, he was more than happy to pay a visit to the senator and update him on the status of his daughter's engagement.

And he planned to do exactly that.

He just needed to make sure his brothers were on board with his entire plan. Because he wasn't stopping there.

Yet again, their father's philandering ways were destroying their lives, but Daniel was putting a stop to it.

He snapped back to the present as Fletcher asked, "What are you suggesting?"

Daniel shared his thoughts and after a robust discussion, they all sat staring at the floor and walls and knew there was little other option. Not when board members and their executive team were already whispering in the corners.

Very few people understood how delicate an organization could be when trust began to flounder. Daniel needed to act fast and aggressively, proving himself to be the powerful CEO he was.

And he fucking was.

No one, not even the founder, and his father, was going to destroy it. Not on his watch.

Daniel picked up his phone and dialed.

"Selena, set up an appointment with Senator Mackenzie for me this afternoon," he instructed his executive assistant. "Then one with my father at 5:00 p.m. In my office."

"Yes, sir."

"Let them both know it's not a request and keep both meetings confidential. Strictly. From everyone," Daniel said, then paused for a moment. "Ask the flight team to prepare my jet for takeoff two hours later. Put me out of the office for two weeks."

He never took leave.

Ever.

Fletcher and Hunter looked up from their phones, their eyebrows shooting to the ceiling. He looked away. Daniel Dufort answered to no one and for once in his life he was doing something for himself.

"As in, out for a vacation?"

"Yes," Daniel replied simply, as he tapped on his photo app and began scrolling through images of Harper. His heart began to beat rapidly in his chest.

God, she's beautiful.

He missed her so fucking much.

"Where shall I tell them you're heading?" Selena asked.

"I'm returning to Honolulu."

It might be too late, but Daniel knew if he didn't try, he'd regret it for the rest of his life.

CHAPTER THIRTY-TWO

"You don't need to decide today or tomorrow, Harp," Kristen said, leaning her face on her hands. "If it's meant to be, it will be. Just get home and clear your head."

They were Facctiming, and Harper had her phone leaning up against a spare cushion while tucking her hands under her pillow. If she wasn't in Hawaii, she would've declared it a duvet day. It was already 10:30 a.m. and she'd been talking to Kristen for over an hour.

Thank you, free penthouse Wi-Fi.

Cooper had walked Harper to her room and wished her goodnight. Then she'd walked into her bedroom and face planted on the bed.

And cried.

When her phone had beeped, Harper had scrambled across the bed to read the message and smiled sadly at Cooper's cute ***goodnight gorgeous lips xx*** message.

Daniel's silence was deafening and painful.

"I feel like I'm about to lose a wonderful man because I'm obsessing over one who doesn't love or want me. I'm insane."

"He *did* say he loved you, though, right?"

Harper flopped onto her back and sighed at the ceiling. "Yes. But he left, Kristen! He left, he hasn't called, and he didn't fight for me."

"You're right," Kristen said and let out her own sigh. "Who knows what he's dealing with back home? It sounds messy and complicated, but I do agree if he truly loved you, he would be fighting for you. Unless he really has to marry this girl and cannot be with you. He might be just as upset as you."

Harper chewed her bottom lip.

"I don't know. He isn't the kind of man to do something he doesn't want. But then again, I don't know his family dynamics. All that money—it makes people do stupid shit."

She turned to face the screen and the two of them frowned in agreement.

"Whatever is going on with Daniel, just know it's okay to still be in love with him. Don't feel bad. He swept you off your feet, honey."

He most certainly had.

"Yeah, he's going to take some getting over," she said.

"For what it's worth, and I'm no love expert, but it sounded like it was the real deal," Kristen said, making her heart ache all over again. "But life doesn't always play fair. I'm sorry, babe."

Harper's eyes moistened.

"Thanks," she said, wiping her eyes, then sat up. "Ugh, I need to get up. I only have one more day on the island. I leave tomorrow morning."

Harper suddenly had a desire to throw herself into the ocean and wash away all this sadness.

"I don't know how I feel about seeing Cooper again, but I will say goodbye to him before I go. I think I just need some time to process everything."

"Things will feel different when you get home."

Home.

A shiver ran through her.

Why did it not feel like home anymore?

Harper shook off the weird vibe.

She said goodbye and then cleared her messages. Two from Cooper and one from *BookFlix*. They had sent her some emails to review, which she responded to after eating a late breakfast in her room.

Finally, she looked at the two from Cooper.

Stop feeling guilty. You did nothing wrong.

Harper smiled. For someone who had just met her, Cooper knew her pretty well.

And good morning, gorgeous. Text me when you wake up. x

It was nearly midday and his messages had landed over four hours ago. She hadn't meant to ignore him for so long, but she'd needed space.

Harper pushed her breakfast plate away and sighed. She was acting as if she had a choice between the two men. She didn't.

Daniel was gone. It had been over twenty-four hours and not a single message. Not even a simple sorry. It was as if everything they'd shared together meant nothing.

Had he truly loved her? Or had this just been a Hawaiian love affair for him?

How could she be so wrong about another man? David had seemed to be fully committed to their relationship, even proposing, and he'd left her for another woman. Her own father had betrayed both her and her mother by building an entirely new family while lying about his loyalty. He'd replaced her with new children.

Tears ran down her face as the familiar childhood pain reared its head.

Whether Daniel wanted to marry this Nadia Mackenzie woman or not, it appeared he was. Once again, another woman was chosen over her.

Daniel had chosen her and not Harper.

It was time to stop being a fool and forget him. Yes, it would take time for her heart to heal, but she was going to stop looking at her phone, waiting for the apology or farewell that was clearly never going to come.

Goodbye, Daniel.

Whether Cooper was the right man for her, only time would tell. Harper would not pursue anything further with him.

She just wanted to get home to New Zealand and if they stayed in touch and he ended up visiting, then so be it.

Now she was going to look after herself.

A few hours later, after a big swim in the ocean and some retail therapy along Kalakaua Avenue, Harper made her way up to *Altitude*. She had a feeling her three amigos would be there.

"Well, well, well," Graydon said, smirking at her when she sat down opposite him sipping on a tall blue cocktail which had about seventy-five cocktail umbrellas and half a pineapple sticking out of it. "Look what the cat dragged in."

Harper grinned at him.

"You really didn't need to go to all the effort," Luke said, referring to her bikini and towel.

"Living the Hawaiian dream. What can I say?" Harper shrugged. She'd quickly noticed people dressed in all kinds of outfits for sunset cocktails. One table could be full of people dressed for a night out while others had come straight from the beach. No one cared.

Harper risked a peek in Cooper's direction. He winked at her, and she smiled. The light had dimmed in his eyes, but it probably had in hers, too.

The four of them talked trash for a few hours while Harper watched the sun sink into the ocean for the last time.

"Man, they never get old." She sighed, taking her last photo of the pink and orange sky.

"You've caught the bug," Cooper said, crunching on some corn chips.

"What bug?"

"The aloha bug. You either love Hawaii, or you don't." He grinned. "You, Harper Kāne, love it."

She couldn't argue with that. It truly was paradise. Her phone buzzed before she could reply.

Daniel.

Fuck.

Her heart pounded. She tucked the phone into her beach bag—she couldn't even bring herself to look at it. No matter what it said, nothing mattered now.

"We're going to *Cheeseburgers in Paradise*," Luke said. "Wanna join?"

Harper shook her head. "I don't. You go ahead and perhaps we can all have breakfast in the morning before I fly out?"

"Deal," Graydon said, and the two of them stood.

"I'll see you down there in a minute," Cooper said, holding her eyes as his friends slapped him on the back and left. He shifted seats so he was sitting opposite her.

"You, okay?" he asked, concern lining his face.

Harper nodded. "I am. Sorry I didn't reply, Coop. I just needed some space to think."

Cooper reached out and took her fingers tentatively in his. "Harper—"

She squeezed them in return, stopping him. "No, please don't make me any promises. When I get home, if you want to stay in contact, that would be nice. Then we can see what happens. No expectations, okay?"

Cooper nodded, looking disappointed, but he forced a smile on his face. "No expectations."

Harper smiled back.

"You *are* an incredible kisser, though," he said.

She shook her head at him and grinned.

"I'll see you for breakfast," Cooper said, standing and kissing her on the top of her head. Then he left to join his friends.

Harper relaxed into her chair and stared up at the sky. She sent out a request to the universe to send her someone to love her, who would make her a priority.

To prove to her it *was* possible.

"Prove to me that real love exists, that I'm worthy of it, and I promise to love that man until my dying breath," she whispered.

CHAPTER THIRTY-THREE

Daniel, Fletcher, and Hunter marched toward Senator Mackenzie's office. Like his brothers, he was top to toe in black. His suit a custom *Tom Ford*. On his wrist was his Patek Philippe (which ironically would single-handedly pay for the extortionist's political campaign). His attitude: pure Dufort.

A few hours ago, his father had attempted to reach him, demanding a reason for being summoned. Daniel hadn't replied.

Johnathan would show up.

"We're here to see Senator Mackenzie," Daniel announced to the flustered receptionist without slowing his walk.

"This way," Fletcher said, and they turned left down the hallway.

Around them, staff began scampering out of their chairs and out behind their desks, like panicked mice.

"Sir, excuse me. Gentlemen, you cannot just go through there," one woman called after them.

Blah, blah, blah.

A secretary sat outside what was obviously the senator's office, but there was no sign on the door. She stood looking panicked.

"Mr. Dufort," she said, her eyes darting to all three of them. "I told Selena the senator is unavailable this afternoon. I'm afraid—"

"I doubt that will be the case for much longer." Daniel scowled and walked right past her. He opened the heavy wooden door and stood in the doorway, flanked by his two just as sizeable and powerful brothers.

He took in the men sitting around a large table.

"Your 3:00 p.m. has arrived, and I think you'll find you've double-booked yourself, Senator," Daniel said, walking into the room. Hunter and Fletcher followed. "See yourself out, gentlemen."

The senator stared at them with outer calm, but Daniel knew he was anything but that. He had to give him points for his composure, but then again, the man was a politician and had many years of deceit under his belt.

Their eyes met and Daniel held his stare with far more chill. The senator twitched. *That's right, asshole, you aren't getting a penny of Dufort money.*

Mackenzie cleared his throat and his eyes drifted back to his guests.

"It appears my secretary *has* double-booked me today," the senator said. "Please accept my apology, my future son-in-law and I have some important business to discuss."

Daniel's jaw tensed.

The man was trying his patience. Out of the corner of his eye, he saw Fletcher roll his eyes, all *fucking jerk.*

Hunter held the door open for the other men who, after shaking hands farewell with the senator, began leaving. Nods were exchanged and then the door closed.

"What the fuck is this about?" the senator growled.

"Sit the fuck down!" Daniel roared.

"Don't you dare speak to me like that, son. Do you know who I am?"

From the other end of the table, Daniel leaned both his hands on the solid wood and narrowed his eyes at the man. "I am not your fucking son and never will be. Now sit. The. Fuck. Down."

He stared at the man for a moment.

"Trust me when I say you do not want anyone outside this room hearing what we have to say, so if you won't sit, I will open the door."

There was a stare down for a few minutes and then the senator sat.

"You have three minutes."

Daniel ignored the heroics and took a seat, Hunter and Fletcher on either side of him.

"Right now, I have expert video techs working on a video proving Suzanne removed the original loan agreement from our vaults," Daniel said, his voice strong and clear.

The senator blinked once, giving away very little, but he began to pale. "So? What does that have to do with me?"

"The agreement shows the correct amount owed from Dufort Hotels, and proof of blackmail."

The senator laughed.

"You think that's enough to stop me? To stop this wedding? It's not, son."

Say son, one more time and I will punch your fucking lights out.

Instead, Daniel grinned. "I also have in my possession a recording of you discussing your plans to use Suzanne and the extortion of Dufort money to fund your run for president,"

The senator glared back at him across the table. Cold as fucking ice. "Obtained illegally. The authoritics can't do anything with it."

Daniel leaned back in his chair and stared at Mackenzie. He was in no hurry to bury this asshole. In fact, he was enjoying it.

"The media and the public can. Am I right, Fletcher?"

Fletcher sat forward. "They'll love it. No one wants a dirty president."

Mackenzie stood up and planted his hands on the back of his chair.

"You kids have no idea what you are talking about. I've been playing this game a lot longer than you. You think they are going to believe any of this?"

"Seriously, man, it's a recording with your voice," Hunter said, shaking his head at the ignorance of the man.

"Whether I leak it in an official Dufort media release saying we've been blackmailed OR anonymously, your name will be tarnished, Mackenzie," Daniel said. "You decide."

"You don't get to negotiate with me, Daniel Dufort," the senator sneered.

Daniel slammed his fist on the table. "You chose to play in my sandpit when you roped my ass into your corrupt bullshit!" he yelled, standing up. "Dufort Hotels will pay the original loan back to you tonight. You have three hours to release a statement saying the engagement is off."

Fletcher and Hunter stood up.

"You are a rogue playboy. The media isn't going to take a word you say seriously," Mackenzie laughed.

"Cool. You willing to bet your chance of becoming the next POTUS on that?" Fletcher asked, shaking his head. "Because if I were you, I wouldn't."

Either way, the senator was fucked. He just didn't know it yet. Josh Hawke would see to that.

"Two hours or I am taking action," Daniel said. "If you try to fuck with me, my family or my business again, I will fucking bury you."

Mackenzie plunged his hands into his pockets.

"One day I will be president and we will have quite a different conversation, son. Mark my words."

Daniel laughed.

"You've forgotten one thing, Senator. Presidents aren't born, they are made by powerful and rich men. Men like me. I am a billionaire in my own right, many times over. I have influence in corners of this country and around the world you couldn't even dream of."

Daniel walked to the door and turned. "No, sir, you will never be President of the United States. I will make sure of it."

"That recording—"

"Send the release and it will be destroyed," Daniel replied, and they both knew it wouldn't be. Daniel would lock it in his personal vault. He lived in a world where information was power, and it wasn't the only thing he had tucked away in there.

"I know my father is ultimately responsible for this," Daniel said. "You've had your revenge. Now move on."

"I have not had my fucking revenge," the man said, his jaw tense.

"Well, you need to get over it. I'm in charge of the Dufort Dynasty now, so you two can slap dicks in another playground," Daniel said, turning away. "This conversation is over."

"Two hours," Fletcher reminded him, tapping his Rolex. Then the three of them walked out of the building and stood on the sidewalk, turning to face one another. There were a couple of smirks, even though Daniel's blood was still pumping.

"I thought that went rather well," Hunter said.

Daniel let the corners of his lips curl.

He still had one more meeting, and it was going to be much more difficult.

CHAPTER THIRTY-FOUR

Daniel stood in his office looking out across Central Park, waiting for his father to arrive. He had one hand in his pocket and the other holding his phone.

He stared at the screen.

I should text her.

Every time Daniel thought about what to say, it sounded wrong. It sounded like bullshit. Much of what had happened with the extortion, he could never share with Harper, but he knew he'd have to trust her with *some* information to buy back her trust.

All of which he could only do in person, not over the phone.

Daniel trusted Harper to keep the information confidential, but for her safety, there was only so much he would tell her.

Daniel hoped like hell she would give him an opportunity to explain and give him a chance.

Another one.

He wasn't a religious man, but for the first time in his life, talking to God was on the tip of his tongue.

Nothing made sense now he was home, and Harper wasn't in his arms anymore. Yes, his family and the business were important, but there was room in his life for the woman he loved.

Dufort Hotels was a part of him. One part. The other was a man who loved Harper Kāne with everything he was.

He was going to move mountains to win her back.

"Why aren't you answering my calls?" His father's angry voice broke through his thoughts.

Daniel pocketed his phone and turned.

"Please sit," Daniel said, pushing a whisky across the meeting table at his father, and sitting down in his own chair. He was greeted with an angry stare for a few minutes, but Daniel ignored it, tipping his glass to his lips.

"What is this all about?"

Even though a fire burned within him, Daniel felt some sadness about what he was about to say. God knows this had never been in his long-term life plan.

"As of two hours ago, you're no longer president of Dufort Hotels," Daniel said calmly.

"What the hell are you talking about?" his father growled.

"We called an emergency board meeting, and your absence was noted."

His father stood, fury pouring off him.

"Wha—are you joking? You've run a coup?!" Johnathan Dufort yelled.

Daniel tossed his drink back and slammed it on the table. "No, Father, I did what was necessary to remove the greatest risk to this company. You! I did my fucking job."

He stood, walked to the side cabinet, and poured another whisky.

"What the hell are you talking about, Daniel?"

Daniel turned and pointed at him with the cut crystal glass. "I cleaned up your God damn mess with Mackenzie and Suzanne. I took my fucking life back. One you were quite happy to bargain with to save your own ass," his voice raised.

Jonathan waved his arm around as he paced. "I was being blackmailed. What would you have had me do? Anyway, this is *my* damn company. You can't kick me out, son."

Not anymore.

"It hasn't been yours for a long time. Not since you listed, and certainly not when you did *fuck all* to find a solution to *our little problem.* Did you even try? Or did you know this entire time this was payback for being caught with his wife?"

His father paled.

"Don't worry," Daniel said. "I don't want details or to know anything more. You're womanizing and the harm it caused my mother, our family and this business is over, Dad."

Jonathan scoffed angrily. "Grow up, Daniel. This is life. This is what men do. In any case, you can't just vote me out. I own the majority shares of Dufort Dynasty. It's *my* name on this building and our hotels."

No, it wasn't what all men did. It wasn't what he was going to do once he had Harper back in his arms. He had no interest in any other women. If she wouldn't have him, he did not know what he'd do.

Go back to emotionless fucking.

No thanks.

She was it for him.

"The board voted," he said, and there was dead silence as the two powerful Dufort men stared at each other.

Daniel had loved and respected his father all his life and while he was angry at him, he still felt a strong sense of disappointment that it had come to this.

Hell, Johnathan was willing to marry off one of his sons, or let the business pay out billions of dollars to pay off their blackmailer. It would have destroyed them.

All because he couldn't keep his cock in his pants.

Worse, he'd not been honest with Daniel or made any effort to fix this. His promises and words had all been bullshit.

"Suzanne has spoken up about your sexual relationship in exchange for dropping charges against her. You have breached multiple company policies and put Dufort Hotels and our shareholders at risk," Daniel finished. "Between the three of us, Fletcher, Hunter and I have the majority shareholding and vote."

It had been a big day as all three of them cashed in their shares and funds to make this happen.

Jonathan's eyes dropped.

"Well," he said, "I see I have taught you well. In a way, I'm actually proud of you."

"The money will be in your account in a few hours," Daniel added. "You will retain ten percent shares, which gives you some voting rights and…hell, Dad, you know this shit. You taught me."

Johnathan nodded and sent him a sad smile. Then let out a dry laugh.

"God. I never meant for it to come to this, but I felt cornered."

Daniel nodded.

"You should have been honest with me."

"Fuck, I know," he said, shaking his head. "I am glad the business is in your hands. The three of you have always been close."

Of course they had—all they'd had was each other. Their father had never been around unless he was teaching them the business, and he had done an excellent job at that.

Teaching them to be good men? That had yet to be seen.

Teaching them to be good husbands? No, but it didn't mean the Dufort men couldn't do things differently now.

"We had to be," Daniel said, turning to the windows and the lights of Manhattan. "I am sorry, Dad. I want you to know that none of us wanted this, but you won't change. You never did for Mom, or for us. Hell, you were willing to let me marry a woman I didn't even like, let alone love."

"You know nothing about love, son."

Daniel turned and stared coldly at his father.

"No, Dad, *you* know nothing about love." He dropped his glass on his desk, picked up his laptop and wallet, then walked to the door, holding it open. He'd had enough. "I'll see you out."

Daniel was clear on his priorities now. The Dufort Dynasty was in his hands, and he would let no one destroy it.

And once he had Harper back, no one and nothing would come between them ever again.

If he won her back.

Fletcher and Hunter waited in the hallway, and after an uncomfortable silence, his father stepped out and stood in front of them.

"As unhappy as I am about this, I am proud of you all for sticking together and using your heads," he said. "Is Mackenzie dealt with?"

"Yes. A media release has just arrived in my inbox," Fletcher said, his eyes also darting to Daniel.

He gave Fletcher a nod.

They made their way downstairs and stood watching as their father's car drove away.

"Fuck me," Hunter said, rubbing the stubble on his face.

"He's going to be furious when the shock wears off," Fletcher said. "You know he won't let this go, right?"

Daniel nodded. "I know."

Fletcher was right. His father had built this company with his bare hands. It was his life's work. He was a smart and strategic man. There was no way he thought his father had just accepted what had happened tonight and was going home to plan his golf game for the next twenty years.

"We don't want to be at war with him," Hunter said.

"Well, that's up to him, but either way, we had to protect the company," Daniel said. "He's not out, just less able to fuck things up now."

Daniel tightened his scarf around his neck.

"I've got to go," he said when he spotted his driver pull up. "It's a shit time to leave. I'm sorry, but this is important. Call me if there are any emergencies, otherwise you two are in charge for two weeks."

Fletcher smirked.

"We'll be fine," Hunter said. "You do fuck all. We all know that."

Daniel laughed.

"Fletcher, keep your mitts off Olivia," Daniel said, as his brother's smirk dissolved.

He'd deal with that when he returned. Right now, Harper was his priority.

He was going to get his girl.

A few hours later, Daniel was in the air. He still had an eleven-hour flight ahead of him, but he was excited to see Harper. And nervous as hell.

He chewed the side of his lip.

Finally, he'd thought of the perfect words to text her and his finger hovered over the send button.

Press it.

I figured out my priorities. It's you, Harper. x

Then he waited.

And waited.

And she never replied.

Fuck.

CHAPTER THIRTY-FIVE

"Houston, we have a problem," Harper said out loud to herself. If only NASA would swoop on in and help her right now.

Her suitcases wouldn't shut.

She hadn't realized how much shopping she'd done over the past two weeks, or quite how much space five pairs of shoes, two hats and three new handbags would take up.

Not that she was in the business of calculating the velocity of…whatever. Stuff just didn't fit.

Crap.

There was no way she was leaving it here. She'd spent a small fortune and loved everything she'd purchased. Then she remembered her favorite item, which she now wished she hadn't brashly returned.

Her Cartier watch.

She loved it.

Not because of its value, but the meaning and memories of her time with Daniel.

She'd finally looked at his message this morning, then stared at it for ten minutes as her heart pounded. Harper didn't know what it meant. Eventually she had put her phone down, remembering he was good with words. He'd told her he loved her, but they had also just been words. Without action, there was little substance.

What was he expecting her to say in response? Thank you?

She didn't have anything to say in reply, so chose to wait until she landed in New Zealand.

She flopped on the bed beside her suitcase and looked around the penthouse.

She sighed.

Harper reflected on her vacation. Though it had been a rollercoaster, she'd gained so much clarity about her life here in Hawaii. Looking back, she recognized she'd never been in love with David. In fact, she was grateful he'd left her. Without him setting her free, she may not have secured her tv deal with *BookFlix*, and most certainly wouldn't have experienced the most passionate holiday romance of her life.

To date.

Even through her tears and broken heart, she would never regret a moment with Daniel. She loved him and it would just take time to heal.

Cooper had shown her there were men willing to put a woman first and one day she'd find it. Both of them knew it wasn't with him, but she was glad they had their moment together.

Daniel's text came to mind.

What did it mean?

A tiny bubble of hope rose to the surface. Harper wondered if perhaps the love she and Daniel shared would see them come together again one day.

She wouldn't wait for him, but if Daniel was a man who stood by his words, then he'd show. Not just tell her.

Either way, she was carrying on with her life.

Harper let out a long sigh and glanced at the clock. She had breakfast to attend, and hopefully she could recruit the three amigos to help her with her luggage issues at the end of it.

She raced downstairs and found them in the restaurant as planned.

"Have you started without me?" she said, sitting down next to Graydon and staring at them.

"You're fifteen minutes late." Luke shrugged. "We're growing young men."

She let out a snort. "Hate to break the bad news, but you are all completely grown."

Cooper lifted his arm to expose a deliciously tanned bicep and nodded. "Yup."

Harper laughed and thanked the server as he poured coffee. "Just a muffin and some fruit, please."

"You can't exist on that," Graydon said, then called out, "She'll have eggs, as well."

"I will not." Harper laughed, shaking her head at the laughing Dufort server. "I'm flying in a few hours, so I get nervous. I'm only eating because I'm having breakfast with you three."

Forty minutes later, Harper had recruited them to help with her suitcase issue, and they all stood to head upstairs.

"Ms. Kāne," Akino said, appearing out of nowhere.

"Akino, aloha, how are you?"

"I came to wish you a safe flight home," he said. "I look forward to seeing you later in the year for the *High Stakes BookFlix* launch."

"Mahalo," she said, thanking him. "How lucky am I to be returning to beautiful Hawaii again so soon?"

She glanced up and saw Cooper catch her eye. It had crossed her mind that it might be an opportunity for them to meet up again and pursue things if they kept in contact, but she was making no decisions.

She smiled at him with no hint of commitment and looked away.

"What time is your pick up?" Akino asked.

"Eleven," she said.

He gave her a quick hug and walked away.

Weird.

"If they burst open in the cargo, I will curse your names for the rest of my life," Harper said, staring at her two suitcases, which had just been treated to what could only be described as torture.

But they were shut and had their padlocks on. She was now ready to go home.

Cooper pulled her into a big hug, nearly squishing her. "I'm going to head out," he said into her hair. "This isn't goodbye, Harp. I'll message you tomorrow."

She smiled and kissed his cheek.

The knock at the door interrupted them, and Luke let the porter in. He took one look at her bloated luggage, and they all laughed.

Graydon and Cooper helped the Hawaiian man lift them onto his trolley, and she tipped him a juicy twenty.

"He deserves every dollar of that," Luke said, nodding.

"Okay, you guys, get out of here before I cry," Harper said, hugging them and then they left, promising to stay in touch and wishing her a safe flight.

The door closed and Harper was alone.

She stood looking around the penthouse, empty of all her belongings, awaiting its next guests.

She walked to the sliding doors which led to the lanai and stared out across the sparkling blue waters of Waikiki.

It was another beautiful day in paradise.

Literally.

Memories of the time she'd spent with Daniel from the crazy hurricane, their makeshift meal in the kitchen, to their helicopter flight to Maui came flooding back.

Her eyes filled with tears as all her emotions rose to the surface. God, what was she going to do with all this love she felt for Daniel? Just throw it in the bin? How did people recover from such heartbreak?

She hadn't realized how much being in Hawaii, in his penthouse, was keeping the connection of their relationship alive for her. Once she walked out of the Dufort hotel, it was over.

Her head dropped.

"Harper."

She turned at the sound of her name, and her mouth fell open.

CHAPTER THIRTY-SIX

God, she was the most beautiful thing he'd ever seen.

Ever.

Period.

The simple emerald-green sundress showed off her gorgeous, tanned shoulders and on her feet, she wore a pair of simple white sneakers. To him, she looked like a million dollars.

She also looked like she was about to crumble to the floor.

"Hey," Daniel said, flying across the room and gripping her hips. She stared at him with parted lips as his heart pounded in his chest. "Harper, speak to me."

"What are you doing here?" she whispered.

"You know what I'm doing here, baby," he said and brushed a lock of hair from her forehead. "I'm just praying I'm not too late."

She swallowed and looked around.

"No flowers or grand gestures?"

Daniel smirked. "Okay, in my defense, I had eleven hours to overthink this. I was going to fill the lobby with roses or rent one of those planes to fly over Waikiki Beach with a banner declaring my love. Or I thought about intercepting you at the airport with aloha dancers and a band."

Harper let out a tearful laugh.

"Then I rang my jeweler to organize a ring."

"A ring?" Harper gasped, a tear on the tip of her eyelashes.

"But then I decided when I ask you to be my wife, I am *not* doing it in one of my hotels," he said, capturing the tear.

Harper's lips opened and closed, clearly speechless. Then she swallowed slowly, blinking at him.

There were so many things he wanted to say, but he had to take this step by step. He slipped the Cartier watch back where it belonged and smiled. "You left something in my room."

"Thank you," Harper said, emotion thick in her voice. She looked up and gave him a watery smile.

He took her chin and gazed into her beautiful blue eyes. God, he'd missed them.

"I finally realized what you want from me—no, what you need from me—is to show you how much you mean to me. And I intend to do that."

Another little tear escaped, and he caught it with his thumb.

"You deserve better than how we started, Harper. I lost you because I put everything else before you. I will never do that again. I love you. You are the sole most important thing to me. This is not a promise—I'm going to show you every God damn day of my life."

"Daniel," she said, a little hic in her throat.

"If you'll have me?"

"Are you sure this is what you want?" Harper asked.

"I just flew across the world to tell you, so I'm pretty sure." He smirked. "I know it's going to take some time to earn back your trust, and I'm willing to do everything it takes."

"God, I missed you." She cried, and he pulled her into his arms.

"Can we do this?" he asked, his face buried in her hair. Daniel was a confident man, but he felt his body shiver at the thought of Harper saying no. "Please?"

She nodded.

Daniel pulled back. He had to be sure.

"I mean really do this," Daniel said. "Because I *am* going to ask you to marry me, Harper. When I do, you will *know* my priority is making you the happiest woman alive."

And he would.

Because Daniel Dufort never failed, and he most definitely wasn't failing Harper Kāne—the woman he loved.

CHAPTER THIRTY-SEVEN

Harper sat with her toes in the sand and wiggled them. Beside her, Daniel sat eating a double scoop of chocolate ice cream.

"New Zealand dairy really is incredible. I thought it was just hearsay. God, this is delicious," Daniel said.

She grinned.

They'd spent another day in Hawaii so Daniel could recover from his flight, and then a driver had taken them to a private airfield on Oahu for their flight to New Zealand.

Harper's mouth had dropped open as she took in the large private jet. Inside, it was like a luxurious living room. White and beige leather seats and sofas filled three different spaces and there were at least six crew she had spotted.

At least if her luggage exploded, she wouldn't lose it.

She had tried to act cool, but Daniel had pulled her up against him and said, "It's okay to be overwhelmed by all this, sweetheart. It's going to take some time to adjust. Just be you, okay?"

"Well then, in that case, *fucking hell*," she said and saw one of the crew smile.

The truth was, she didn't know if she'd ever get used to a billionaire lifestyle, but she loved Daniel and they both had some adapting to do.

They'd made love in the bedroom at the rear of the plane and enjoyed a delicious three-course meal during their flight—plus snacks—so Harper thought she'd adjust just fine.

The waves crashed gently on the golden sands in front of her as people swam, played in the sand, and sunbathed in the late summer sun.

A dog ran past them, chasing a seagull, and Harper laughed. She turned to watch Daniel manage his melting ice cream with his skilled tongue, and she grinned.

He raised a brow. "Keep looking at me like that and we're going straight home."

She laughed, and he planted his chocolate-covered lips on hers. Harper giggled and licked her lips clean.

She had a surprise for him. One she knew he would like.

"Speaking of home," she said, and Daniel instantly lowered his ice cream.

"Yes?" he asked, all humor gone from his face.

"Yes," Harper said.

He dropped the ice cream to the sand and twisted to face her. "Yes, yes? Or yes?"

"Yes, I'll move to New York with you," she said, bursting into joyous laughter as Daniel tackled her to the sand and kissed her passionately. Her giggles faded as the weight of his body settled on hers in a possessive and protective manner.

She was his.

Body, mind, and soul.

Over the past few weeks, Daniel had proven she was his everything. He'd walked away from a multi-billion-dollar business to put Harper first, despite some of the mess that was going on.

She knew he hadn't shared everything and understood it was for her protection. The world of politics, money and power was a dangerous one at times—something she'd had to consider while deciding whether to step into his life.

But how could she not?

She loved Daniel with all her heart and couldn't imagine living without him.

Daniel and Kristen had hit it off immediately, and after a night out at one of Auckland's hottest night spots, the two of them had bonded over a love of whisky. That Daniel could buy them all the best of the best had helped, but Harper had just sat back and smiled, watching her two favorite people together.

Her mother was a different story.

It was clear to Harper now her mother didn't trust a soul, not even herself. Daniel saw through it and said it was only important to him what Harper felt. And she loved him for it.

However, being the dominant man he was, she should have known Daniel wouldn't just drop it. He invited her mother for a walk after dinner one evening and kissed Harper on the forehead, saying they'd be back soon.

Twenty minutes later, they returned, and a sort of peaceful alliance had been formed. Daniel wouldn't tell her what they'd spoken about, only that he'd promised he would love Harper until his dying breath and make sure she knew every day how much she was loved.

Big words.

This time they came with actions. Daniel had invited her to move to New York. A man who had never had a relationship in his life had asked her to move across the world to live with him.

"I know you need a visa, Harper, and I intend to make you my wife, so don't worry about that," he had said.

She had laid her hand on his arm, shaking her head. "Daniel, I don't need a visa. My father was Hawaiian. I'm half American."

He stared at her.

"I don't want that to be the reason you propose," she had said, and that had gone down badly. She cringed even now, remembering his response.

Daniel's mouth lifted from hers and he grinned at her. "I'm so fucking happy. I can't wait to take you home, sweetheart."

He pulled her to a sitting position and sat back on his heels in the sand.

"If I hate the snow, I'm going to Hawaii for the winter," Harper said, giving him a grin. "And I don't know how big your wardrobe is, but I want half."

Daniel laughed.

She already knew his apartment in New York was enormous. He'd shown her photos and told her a lot about what to expect. Some of it she knew was to get her prepared and some to incentivize her.

Harper didn't need any of it.

She just wanted Daniel. To feel his eyes on hers, his body against hers every night, and to wake with him in the morning.

And all the delicious parts in between.

"I think you might find I can accommodate both those requests. Anything else?"

"I'm going to keep writing. I'm not going to become one of those kept women," Harper said. It was important she keep her independence.

He frowned. "Hmm, see, now we have a problem."

Harper's eyes widened.

"I don't want you to be a kept woman either, but I want you to be my wife," Daniel said, cupping her face, and their two sets of blue eyes met.

"Marry me." He said, pure love beaming from his eyes. "Marry me, Harper. Be my wife and spend forever with me."

"Yes," Harper replied, her own eyes filling with joy.

CHAPTER THIRTY-EIGHT

Daniel woke and stretched but felt something warm wrapped around him.

His fiancée.

"Mmm mmm," she mumbled.

They were both adjusting to all the flying and time zone changes, and the fact that Hunter and Fletcher had showed up with a bottle of champagne when they'd flown in yesterday to celebrate their engagement.

In hindsight, he should've kept her to himself a little longer, but they'd told Kristen and Harper's mother, and he wanted to share the joyful news with his brothers.

Of course, they had loved her immediately and told her a bunch of outright lies about him. Harper had laughed while snuggled up against him on the sofa. He'd ignored the smirks from his brothers.

He'd tell his parents in a few days. For now, he wanted to use the last few days he had before returning to the office to show Harper around Manhattan and get her settled in.

"I'm going to hire you some help," he had said.

"Help for what?" Harper had asked.

"Setting up bank accounts and all the legal stuff of moving to a new country. It's a lot of work and having someone to take the stress off will help."

"What if I want you to help?" she'd asked.

"Then I will," Daniel had answered. "But I do have a business to run, and wouldn't you rather our time together be a bit more enjoyable than paperwork?"

She had melted into his body and nodded. "Yes, but it still feels weird."

"Welcome to money," he'd said. "Where you get to outsource the crap in life you don't want to do, while providing income for others."

Harper had mulled that over, then agreed an assistant would be helpful while she adjusted to her new life in America.

They had decided to have a late summer wedding but were yet to decide on a location.

He rolled toward her, and Harper blinked her eyes open. "Good morning, Mrs. Dufort."

"Not yet," she replied, her voice all crackly. "I think I lost a toe last night. It's so cold here."

Daniel smirked. "I'd sew it back on if you did. That's how much I love you." Then the smile he loved appeared on her face. "Are you happy?"

She nodded. "You? Does this freak you out as much as you thought it would?"

"No," he said, running his hand over her backside and lifting her leg over his. His hard cock rubbed against the warmth between her legs. "Coming home without you felt wrong."

Her mouth fell open as Daniel pressed inside.

"Fuck, baby," he groaned.

Gripping her ass, he moved rhythmically, giving Harper time to adjust to his morning greeting. She dug her fingers into his upper chest and arched into him.

"Mmphhhf, oh, God, yes, more, deeper," she said.

He flipped them, pulling Harper under him and her legs around him. Then plunged inside her to the hilt. Her pussy clenched around him.

"Yes, yes," Harper cried.

He loved seeing pleasure and ecstasy on the face of the woman he was going to marry. Despite what he'd already achieved in his life, making Harper happy every day was the thing Daniel was most proud of.

She was soon to be a Dufort and would be part of their dynasty. He would give her everything she wanted and more.

Daniel felt her body tremble as she began to orgasm. Daniel lifted her to him. "Fuck, I love you."

"Oh, God, I love you," Harper cried as his seed poured into her.

Despite everything, both of them had overcome their fear of commitment and love.

Daniel would make sure their children knew what true love looked like, because his love for Harper was unbreakable.

Turn the page to read Forbidden Touch, Book two in the Dufort Dynasty. Or buy now books2read.com/ForbiddenTouch-Dufort

FORBIDDEN TOUCH

CHAPTER ONE

Fletcher stood at the front of the room in his luxury triplex penthouse and stared out at the hundred or so guests. Behind all the bow ties and cocktail dresses, the lights of Manhattan skyscrapers twinkled brightly

"To Daniel and Harper," he said, lifting his glass of whisky, finishing his toast to the newly engaged couple.

The crowd echoed his words, and the music started, as his eldest brother scooped up his bride-to-be and planted his lips on hers. This was now a common occurrence since Daniel had arrived back in New York three weeks ago with the pretty New Zealander. The two lovebirds had met in Hawaii while Daniel was there on business.

Harper giggled, and then they were surrounded by well-wishers. Above her head, Daniel mouthed *thanks, Fletch.*

Fletcher liked Harper.

She was sassy, strong, and had a huge heart. More importantly, she loved his big brother and didn't let him get away with any of his dominating shit. Daniel needed someone strong, and he'd most certainly found her.

Whether that continued into the bedroom, he really didn't want to know, but from the doe eyes he saw from Harper, he highly doubted it.

Fletcher accepted a fresh glass of whisky from the waiter and made his way across the room. He'd offered to host the intimate engagement party at his apartment so the two could disappear when they wanted. Plus, he knew how private Daniel was about his personal space, and Harper was still settling in. Not just to a new home and country, but a billionaire lifestyle.

While most people would roll their eyes at such a thought—and Fletcher had been born with a silver spoon in his mouth—he could still understand it was a huge change.

Now she had a driver, personal security, and staff in her home most days. The media was desperate to know her, so when Harper refused to give interviews, they'd done what they did best. Made it up.

Fletcher had completed his master's in communications, and as CMO—chief marketing officer—of Dufort Hotels, he knew the games the media played very well.

He'd sat down with Harper, along with his PR Manager, Olivia, to talk her through a handful of options, but she hadn't wanted to talk to them. Understandable, even if it wasn't the best option. Daniel had said it was her decision and supported her either way. If she didn't want to be in the spotlight, Harper didn't need to be.

She had, however, hit it off with Olivia immediately. It hadn't altogether surprised him. Olivia was smart, funny and…totally off limits to him.

He was her boss and, well, a majority shareholder in the Dufort Dynasty. Plus, there was the pesky policy about not fornicating with staff.

Or running your eyes over their ass, but you seem to be happy doing that.

It was something they'd put in place when Daniel had become CEO two years ago. Their father had a poor history of not keeping his cock in his pants—a fact their mother had learned after drinking herself crazy for many years. So had their many human resource managers who constantly quit on them.

Johnathan Dufort had built a multi-billion-dollar dynasty, but he was a liability.

Which was why, after being dragged into an extortion attempt by a US senator, because of their father's philandering ways, Daniel had run a coup. It meant Johnathan now had fewer shares and less control over the business. Protecting them all. Shareholders included.

Fletcher and Hunter had supported Daniel's decision, and now the three collectively held the majority shares.

The board wasn't happy, but after hearing *some* of the details about the blackmail, where Daniel was being coerced into marrying a senator's daughter because of past history between the two men, they agreed to it.

The relationship with their father was tense, but not angry. Across the room he stood talking to a few of the Dufort board members who had been invited. It would be wise of them all not to underestimate their very smart father.

"Great evening, Fletch," someone said, clinking glasses with him as they made their way to the kitchen.

Fletcher was used to hosting parties, so it had been no big deal to pull it together last minute. Or so his executive assistant had said.

"Fletch, man, how are you?" Trevor, a family friend, asked as he sidled up beside him.

"Good, buddy. So glad the timing worked out. I know you're a busy man. Dan's happy you could make it," Fletcher said, slapping him on the shoulder.

Hunter, his younger brother, joined them. "Trev, are you leaving? We're heading over to *Joy Club* afterwards. Join us?" Hunter asked.

Joy Club. Yeah, it was exactly as it sounded and not Fletcher's scene at all.

The man shook his head. "Can't. I have a big presentation tomorrow, so I need to get a few hours' sleep in."

Trevor was a medical researcher with a focus on infectious diseases. Though he was young, he was making great strides in his career already.

"On a Saturday?" Fletcher asked, even though he was guilty himself of working outside normal business hours. They had hotels all over the globe, including Australia, England, Europe, and the United States, so while most of the time his large marketing team in their head office connected with the local teams at weird hours because of the time zones, at times he would join them. Or simply be working on strategy and budgets.

All the boring shit he never had envisaged.

Still, he loved what he did and couldn't imagine doing anything else.

"Hey, I'm still working on my first billion, Dufort," Trevor joked. "But yeah, a fucking Saturday."

They all knew Trevor was never going to starve. His whole family was made up of medical professionals.

"If I said we had a private room booked, would that sway you? It's been a couple of years, dude. Come on," Hunter said, tapping Trevor on the arm with his crystal tumbler.

Fletcher grinned and turned away to leave them to their conversation.

There were two years between each of the Dufort brothers and when Daniel had befriended Trevor at Harvard, he'd joined them for some of the holidays. Hunter may have been the youngest, but the two of them had bonded over their common interest in some kinky shit.

Totally not Fletcher's thing.

Not that he was a vanilla lover—not at all. But whips and stuff? Nope.

Hunter had always been a control freak, so he could only imagine—though he tried not to—what he was like in the bedroom. Or wherever he fucked.

"Next time, Hunt," Trevor replied, slapping him on the shoulder. "Enjoy, but right now I better go say goodbye to Daniel. Harper's awesome, right?"

Both of them nodded.

"She's perfect for him," Fletcher said, sipping his whisky as he watched her run her hand mindlessly up and down Daniel's chest. She had a dreamy look in her eyes and when he glanced at his brother, he saw the look was mirrored.

Who would have thought?

A Dufort brother getting married.

After what they'd seen their mother be put through, all three of them had said a hard no to matrimony *not-bliss*.

At thirty, Fletcher was in no hurry to even think about it. Like most men in his position, he had a lot of choices when it came to women. He was rich, *fucking good looking,* to quote *Forbes* magazine, with a large muscular body. All three of them had similar physiques with dark hair, but where Daniel had freaky light blue eyes, his were green.

They'd gotten their looks from their father and God knows the man had put his to good use over the decades.

Buzz, buzz.

Fletcher slipped his hand inside his grey Tom Ford jacket and pulled out his phone.

Olivia.

His cock twitched.

God

damn it.

New York Daily News is asking for an exclusive on the launch. Yes? No?

Fletcher flipped his wrist and glanced at his Patek Philippe. Ten damn o'clock. What the hell was Olivia doing working on the media for the *Dufort Soho* launch this late on a Friday night?

Liv, shut down your laptop and have a drink. Or go dancing. NYDN can wait until Monday.

And they could. The launch of their new luxury hotel in Manhattan was a week away, which was an eternity in the media world.

Yeah, yeah, I'm leaving soon. I have a demanding boss.

Fletcher snorted.

Wait. Was she still at the office?

He pressed call.

"Fletcher," Olivia purred.

Okay, she didn't purr, but in his head she had. Like a damn sex kitten.

He stepped away from the crowd and walked through his penthouse to the private dining room. He left the lights off and stepped up to the floor-to-ceiling glass.

Three stories of glass.

"Why are you still there?" he asked, purring back.

Olivia groaned. Like actually did.

He squeezed his eyes shut as his cock began to stand to attention.

"I wanted to lock in all the media before Monday. Next week is going to be busy, and I get Sammy back on Sunday night."

And now things were heading back downtown.

Sammy was Olivia's five-year-old daughter. A little mini-me. Flaming red hair that curled haphazardly around her head with bright blue eyes.

"It'll be fine. You need to start delegating to Katy and Thomas more."

"Not this stuff, you know I can't," she said, and he could tell by her voice she was distracted packing up. "Anyway, how many bosses ring to tell their staff off for working late?"

The corners of Fletcher's lips curled.

He put the call on speaker and sent off a text.

"I haven't done a survey, so I can't answer that, but I've just sent Frederick your way, so he will be downstairs in five minutes. He's driving you home."

"Fletcher," she said in a little growl.

He smiled.

"Don't argue. I'm your boss, remember?"

"I can take the subway just like the rest of New York."

Yeah, no, fuck that.

He hated Olivia using the subway at all, but it wasn't his place to say anything. But working this late in his company? No, he was crossing the line and making sure she got home safe.

"Don't leave him hanging. You know he hates it," Fletcher said, staring out at the lights with his phone back on his ear and his other hand in his pants pocket.

He knew right now she was scrunching up her nose and silently mouthing something rebellious. They had worked closely together for nearly a year, so he knew her pretty well. Although recently Olivia had invaded his thoughts more and more, and he realized he didn't know all that much.

She had a daughter.

He'd hired her, so he knew she had extensive media and public relations experience in the hotel and tourism industries.

He knew she was single.

At least he thought she was single.

He knew she was unmarried and shared custody of Sammy with her ex.

Fletcher didn't know how she spent her time outside of work, except for the obvious requirements of being a mom.

She let out another groan and then said, "Thank you. See you Monday."

"Olivia," he said. Fletcher didn't know what he was going to say. He just didn't want to hang up.

There was a long silence before she replied.

"Yes?" she whispered

Shit. Shit. Shit.

"Have a good weekend," Fletcher replied finally.

Buy Fletcher and Olivia's steamy billionaire romance now!

books2read.com/ForbiddenTouch-Dufort

BOOKS BY JULIETTE N. BANKS

www.juliettebanks.com

The Dufort Dynasty
Steamy billionaire romance
Sinful Duty
Forbidden Touch
Total Possession

The Moretti Blood Brothers
Steamy paranormal romance

The Vampire Prince
The Vampire Protector
The Vampire Spy
The Vampire's Christmas
The Vampire Assassin
The Vampire Awoken
The Vampire Lover
The Vampire Wolf
The Vampire Warrior

Realm of the Immortals
Steamy paranormal fantasy romance
The Archangel's Heart
The Archangel's Star
The Archangel's Goddess

Printed in Great Britain
by Amazon

84735528R10181